KEEP HOLLY CLOSE

BOOK TWO IN THE REMEMBER ME SERIES

AMANDA RADLEY

SIGN UP TO WIN

Firstly, thank you for purchasing *Keep Holly Close* I really appreciate your support and hope you enjoy the book!

Head over to my website and sign up to my mailing list to be kept up to date with all my latest releases, promotions, and giveaways.

www.amandaradley.com

KEEP HOLLY CLOSE

CHAPTER ONE

"No." Victoria slid the page proofs across the desk to Gideon Fisher.

He softly sighed and picked them up.

She examined the next set of proofs. These had been back to the art department no fewer than eight times, but something still wasn't right. She squinted and noticed the hitch. She put them on the desk and slid them towards her director of photography.

"Also, no."

She moved on to the next set. Gideon wisely didn't ask what was wrong with either set. He'd worked with her long enough to know not ask superfluous questions when she was very clearly in a bad mood.

She expected her team to be able to do their jobs. If she was required to spoon-feed them every single detail, then they'd be better off looking for employment elsewhere. As the editor-in-chief of the most popular fashion magazine in North America, Victoria Hastings had impeccable standards. Anyone who worked at *Arrival* deserved to be there, or they found themselves out of the door very quickly.

Her phone gently rumbled on the desk. She snatched it up and glanced at the screen. It was from Holly, reminding her to issue an invite to Gideon for dinner the following week.

Holly was very insistent that they socialise with people outside of work. Victoria didn't really grasp why. She saw Gideon all day every day; why she now had to see him across the dining room table in her own home baffled her.

It wasn't that she didn't like Gideon. She enjoyed his company very much. If her arm was twisted, she may even have to admit that she liked the after-work dinners. It was just new, and Victoria wasn't always a fan of new.

However, she was a fan of Holly Carter, and that had changed Victoria's perceptions on many things over the last year.

She put her phone back on the desk, face down.

"Holly would like you to come to dinner next week, if you're free."

"Holly would like?" Gideon asked, playfully.

"We would like," she corrected herself. She looked up at him over the top of her glasses. "You know what I mean."

"I'll check my schedule," he teased. "I have a lot of proofs to redo because my boss is being even more demanding than usual."

Victoria rolled her eyes. "Well, do let me know as soon as you can. And I'm not being more demanding than usual; my standards are as high as they were last week, last month, or even last year. It's other people who insist on letting their own standards lapse."

"Don't tell me standards are lapsing!" a newcomer announced.

Her head snapped up to see who had marched into her office without invitation, but any hint of annoyance vanished the second she saw who it was. She smiled, removed her glasses, and stood up. "Steven, how lovely to see you. Back from Switzerland so soon?"

Steven Goodfellow was one of the very few people able to breeze past her two assistants in the outer office and come straight into her inner sanctum. His charming persona allowed him to get away with an awful lot that would have other people on the receiving end of an icy glare.

Steven was finance director for Oculous, the media company that owned *Arrival* Magazine. Victoria had enjoyed a short fling with him many moons before, and they'd managed to maintain a very pleasant working friend-ship ever since.

"Good to see you, Steven." Gideon got up to shake hands with him.

"I'm not interrupting, am I?" Steven held wrapped gifts in his hands, so he used his head to indicate the door through which he had just barged. "I can come back later."

"You're never interrupting," Victoria reassured him. "Besides, I can see you have gifts. The bearer of gifts is always welcome."

Steven leaned over the table, and Victoria leaned forward in response. They shared cheek kisses.

"These are nothing much. Just little things I picked up for Hugo and Alexia," Steven said. "And, of course, a little something for you. Nothing much. What do you buy the woman who has everything?"

"I ask myself the same thing every year," Gideon said. He took the opportunity of Steven's arrival to snatch up the print proofs from the desk. "I'll leave you to it. Great to see you, Steven."

Victoria watched Gideon make his escape, the wide grin on his face indicating relief at being able to cut their production meeting short. She supposed she couldn't blame him; she was in a terrible mood following the problems with the photoshoot that morning. And maybe she had been a little finicky with some of the proofs. Not that she'd ever admit it to him.

"Did I release a rabbit from the trap?" Steven asked, taking a seat in front of her desk.

"Yes, but don't worry. He'll be recaptured before long." She sat down and regarded Steven properly.

He wore a smart, tailored, faded blue twill suit with a matching waistcoat. The white shirt underneath was unbuttoned at the collar, as Steven abhorred wearing a tie. His thick brown hair showed no sign of thinning, and his tanned skin showed no sign of aging. He was as he had been for the last twenty years.

"How are you?" Victoria asked. "You look well."

"I'm very well. *Arrival Switzerland* has finished acquiring its main competitor, so the folks upstairs are naturally very happy."

"I'm sure they are. How long were you there again?"

"Eight months. I came home for a brief time at Christmas, but it was only a flying visit. How are you? The children?" He gestured to the gifts on the table. "I nearly got

Hugo a Swiss Army knife, but I remembered your rule about him not being allowed to play with weapons as a child. Do I get bonus points for that?"

Victoria chuckled. Her fling with Steven had been over before it had really begun, but he had always been interested in the children. It was an interest that continued long after they returned to just being work colleagues and something she deeply appreciated.

"Possibly. I'll reserve judgement until after I see what you *did* get him. In answer to your question, I'm well. The children are, too; Hugo just turned sixteen, and I honestly have no idea how that happened. Just the other minute he was my little boy, and now he's practically a man."

Steven laughed. "And Alexia? Still ruling the roost?"

"Very much so."

"She's nine now, isn't she?" Steven asked, clearly already knowing the answer as he shook his head in astonishment. "How do they grow up so fast?"

"I have no idea; I've been demanding they stop for a while." Victoria sucked in her cheek. She needed to tell him. He was a close friend, probably one of her closest. It had been a while since they'd seen each other, and her news wasn't the kind you shared over email.

"I'm seeing someone," she confessed bluntly.

He grinned and then opened his mouth, pretending to appear scandalised. "Victoria Hastings," he admonished. "You didn't say anything."

"It was a... unique situation," she explained. "And it all happened rather quickly."

"Well, now you've piqued my interest." He pulled his

chair forward and leaned on the edge of her desk. "Tell me everything."

She chuckled and shook her head. "You're ridiculous."

"And you're stalling. Who is he?"

Victoria swallowed. "She, actually."

"Sorry, how heteronormative of me," he said. "Who is *she?*"

Steven had always been open-minded and kind-hearted. She licked her lips and leaned in a little closer, aware that the door to her office was open and that her assistants loved to eavesdrop.

"You won't believe me," she said softly.

He grinned wider. "This is going to be good."

"Do you remember my former assistant, Holly Carter?"

He nodded. "The girl who left you in Paris, I remember."

He appeared to be waiting for the next sentence. She looked at him meaningfully.

He sat upright; confusion painted his expression. "Holly?" He pointed to the outer office. "Holly Carter? The... your... assistant?"

"My *former* second assistant. I know, it's bizarre." She smiled, enjoying his utter bemusement. "Have I shocked you?"

"A little," he admitted. "When you said Holly Carter, I thought you were going to say you met someone connected to her. I thought she vanished?"

"Well, she did." Victoria got up and walked around her desk to close the office door. The mental image that Louise and Claudia were contorting themselves around their desks in an effort to lean closer to the door wouldn't leave her mind.

Steven's gaze followed her around the room. His jaw hung open, and his eyes were wide and confused.

"As you know, Holly disappeared from my side at Paris Fashion Week two years ago. Last year, I was back in Paris and had forgotten all about her," Victoria lied.

Forgetting about Holly Carter had been impossible, although she refused to admit that to anyone. The sudden disappearance of her assistant had been a shock, causing her a great deal of unexpected pain. Not knowing why she had left or where she had gone had played on Victoria's mind for a number of months.

She took Gideon's seat beside Steven. "I'll cut a long story short; it came to my attention that Holly had never left Paris. She'd been involved in some horrific accident and then been carted off to a hospital. In short, Steven, she had… well, has… amnesia."

Steven closed his eyes, shook his head, and then opened them wide, staring at Victoria in obvious amazement. "Amnesia?"

"Yes. She couldn't remember a thing: who she was, why she was in Paris, what had happened to her."

"And none of that has come back?"

"No, she has the odd sense of déjà vu every now and then but nothing concrete. Most likely she will never remember hard facts about her life before the accident."

"Do you know what happened to her?" Steven asked.

"Some kind of accident resulting in brain trauma," Victoria answered. She batted the point away with a flick of her wrist. "Anyway, via this French journalist, I managed to find her and brought her home to New York. It was all completely innocent at the time, but it blossomed into so much more."

"And now you're... together?" Steven questioned.

Victoria almost felt sorry for him; the more she explained, the more confounded he seemed.

"Yes. We live together; we have for almost a year. It was platonic at first, of course. When we first came back from Paris nothing was happening, but it grew into something else. And I don't mind admitting that I... well, I think she's the one." Victoria hadn't admitted that out loud before. It felt strange to hear the words leave her mouth. Strange but wonderful.

Steven's bamboozlement continued.

Victoria looked at him passively, waiting for him to catch up with what she'd been saying.

He shook away the cobwebs and smiled. "Wow, that's wonderful. I'm really happy for you. Wouldn't have seen that coming, but... wow!"

"You'll have to come over to dinner one night. I'd love for you to meet her. Well, meet her again. Did you ever meet Holly? I presume you did?" Victoria stood up and returned to her own chair. She was aware that this short, unscheduled meeting was no doubt already squeezing out another. She glanced at her laptop, checking her planner.

"I'm sure I did," Steven said, "but it was a while ago, and you go through assistants like I go through socks."

She gave him an exasperated look before returning her attention to her screen.

"It must be strange to be in a relationship with someone

who doesn't remember…" He trailed off, seemingly struggling to find the right words.

"What a monster I was to her?" Victoria questioned.

"No! I mean, does she not remember anything from before the accident? Or the accident itself?"

"Not a thing." Victoria clicked away a couple of reminders.

"How strange that she was still in Paris. Didn't we all assume she'd had a moment of madness and just left her post?" Steven asked.

"Yes. She walked away, and later her things were gone. We don't know what happened precisely, but we assumed that she made the decision to leave, packed up her belongings, and then… something happened. We all thought she had been mugged. She's never been the best judge of a location; the idea around the office was that she was probably walking through the roughest area of Paris in her Louboutins."

Victoria could understand Steven's curiosity regarding Holly's amnesia, but she really wished that he would focus a little more attention on the fact that she was in a loving and happy relationship. Then again, he wasn't the first person who had wanted a full blow-by-blow account of the entire series of events.

The conversation with her sister, and later her mother, flashed into her memory. She blew out a frustrated breath. Her sister was still convinced Holly was a gold digger and completely refused to come and meet her in person.

"It's a crazy old world," Steven said.

"It is," she agreed. "But in this case, I won't complain about the results."

"You sound happy," Steven commented, a smile on his face.

"I am. For the first time in a long time, I feel fulfilled." Victoria wasn't going to elaborate. A declaration of love, in her office, in the middle of a Tuesday afternoon, was quite enough.

He smiled again, seeing right through her façade. "That's fantastic news, Victoria. It really is. I'm so busy at the moment with the move back to the city, but once I'm unpacked, I will be in touch. We will have that dinner, and I will get all the gossip from the lovely Holly."

"See that you do. It's been far too long since we've had time to talk properly."

The muffled sound of people gathering by her office door indicated that the attendees of her next meeting had arrived.

"That's my cue." Steven pushed himself up from the chair. "I'll be in touch soon, have a delightful meeting." He laughed heartily, knowing full well that none of her meetings were ever anything less than a test of her patience and endurance.

She allowed herself a small chuckle. Seeing Steven was a lovely respite from her day of terrible meetings. A respite that was now, sadly, over.

He opened the door and greeted some people in the outer office; she could hear him wishing them good luck. She shook her head before removing all trace of emotion from her face.

"Please, do continue to stand idly in my doorway. I'll thoroughly enjoy shouting myself hoarse so you can all hear me," she drawled quietly, knowing that everyone would hear her and jump to attention.

She looked at her watch and already knew she'd be a little late getting home that evening, something that she had been trying and failing to avoid. The meeting attendees quickly filed into the room, and Victoria put her glasses back on.

"Now, in as few words as possible, explain to me how we're going to rescue the abomination you previously presented."

CHAPTER TWO

HOLLY PEERED into the large saucepan with trepidation. It was a new recipe, one she thought sounded easy but that had become a lot more complicated as she progressed through the recipe. Holly had taken to making the family dinner at least three times a week, with varying levels of success.

She now wished that she hadn't sent Carina home early. The Hastings' housekeeper was a marvel, and Holly knew she'd be able to fix her current sauce issue within a couple of minutes.

She lifted the handle of the wooden spoon and stirred the pasta.

"Has that sauce thickened?" she asked herself with a frown.

"Are you talking to pasta?" Alexia queried as she entered the kitchen, schoolwork clutched in her hands.

"Yes, it's like talking to plants." Holly put the lid back on the pan.

"You talk to plants, too?" Alexia put her homework on

the dining table, dragging a chair out by wrapping her foot around the leg.

"Yes, it helps them to grow," Holly explained. "Don't they teach you anything in school?"

"Nothing about talking to plants. Not yet anyway." Alexia sat down and opened her textbook. "Maybe it will be in the later chapters. Have you heard from Mom yet?"

Holly glanced at the phone laying on the kitchen countertop in case she had missed a notification. She hadn't and shook her head. "No, sorry, nothing yet."

"She's going to miss dinner again, isn't she?" Alexia snatched up a pen and angrily pulled the cap off.

"Probably," Holly admitted. "But you know it gets like this close to the middle of the month. She doesn't want to stay late; she'd rather be here."

"If she really wanted to be here, then she'd be here," Alexia complained, burying her head in her homework.

Holly wiped her hands on a tea towel and considered the mini Victoria across the room. Alexia was like her mother in many ways, but the one major difference was that she wore her heart on her sleeve. Where Victoria needed hours and even days of gentle, subtle cajoling to confess whatever played on her mind, Alexia made it clear immediately what her worries were.

Holly knew that Victoria had reluctantly neglected her family in favour of work for many years. Both Alexia and Hugo had spoken of it, Holly's journals documented it, and even Victoria had practically confessed to it.

After Holly's arrival, things started to change. Victoria made more of an effort to be home for dinner, leave at a more reasonable time in the morning, and not work on weekends. Of course, the pushback from *Arrival* was almost immediate. Victoria found herself pulled in both directions, stuck between a family with a new and burgeoning relationship, and a multimillion-dollar company which would be lost without her.

A family meeting ensued at Holly's request. She knew that open lines of communication would be the key. Victoria needed to know that her family wanted to spend quality time with her, but also that they'd support her when that just wasn't possible. And the children needed to know why Victoria had to work such long hours, and that she really would rather be at home.

Victoria had always been overprotective of Alexia and Hugo, effectively shielding them from the negative aspects of life, especially work. Holly used the family meeting to explain to Victoria how that behaviour wasn't helping anyone. The air was cleared, and, for the most part, the children realised and understood that Victoria's insane workload was the reason for her frequent absences.

Even so, Alexia was only nine, and the extremely wise head on her shoulders was sometimes pushed aside by her heart.

Holly lowered the heat on the pasta dish and walked over to the dining table. She sat down opposite the girl and waited for Alexia to stop writing and look up at her.

"Why don't we talk to her about how you're feeling?" Holly suggested.

"What good would that do?" Alexia grumbled.

"I think it would do a lot of good. The last time we spoke it, things got better, didn't they?"

Alexia shrugged. "For a while, I guess."

"Well, adults are forgetful. Sometimes we need reminding of our promises, and sometimes people need to tell us when something is wrong. Now, remember that your mom said she gets really busy when they are closing out the magazine for the month. That's happening right now. So, she might be late getting home, forgetful, and a bit grumpy."

Holly smiled at the memory of the strong and softly spoken Victoria Hastings actively admitting that she was *sometimes* grumpy. Of course, everyone knew it was the case, but to hear Victoria admit it, and apologise for it, had been quietly amusing.

"I know. I just think she's going to go back to the way she was before. And I know the only reason she changed her schedule was because she wanted to spend more time with *you* and keep *you* happy. It didn't have anything to do with us."

Holly flinched. She had had no idea that was what Alexia thought. It was like being doused with a cold bucket of water to realise that this was how the youngest member of the family perceived things.

"Oh, honey, I didn't know you felt that way. That is absolutely not the case," Holly denied. "I might have been the one able to tell her that she needed to change her schedule, but she didn't do it *because* of me. Or to spend more time with *me*. She did it because she wants to see all of us."

Alexia chewed the inside of her cheek thoughtfully.

Holly reached her hand across the table and waited for Alexia to reach out and connect them. She squeezed the girl's hand tenderly. "She loves all of us, but I think you're her favourite," she confessed in a light-hearted whisper. "Hugo and I can't compete."

Alexia giggled.

"But, seriously," Holly said, "your mom loves you and she wants to do what's best for you. She just gets caught up with work sometimes. You need to remind her of the promises she made to help her keep them. And I can guarantee you that your mom didn't simply spend more time at home because of me. I'm sorry you thought that was the case."

Alexia pulled her hand back. "I think I know that. It just seems that way sometimes."

"Well, I'm sorry that it does. That's something your mom and me need to work on. Do you feel left out?" Holly hoped that wasn't the case. She adored spending time with Alexia, and as often as possible the whole family spent time together. But she knew that Victoria's limited free time sometimes meant there wasn't much room for specific mother-daughter activities.

Alexia shrugged. "A little, maybe. Sometimes."

Holly nodded her understanding and filed away a mental note to speak with Victoria about the issue. The doors of communication had been closed for too long in the Hastings house, and Holly would spend as much time as necessary ensuring they were wedged opened again.

"We'll work on that," she promised. Holly's phone rang. "I bet that's her now." She stood up.

"Bet it isn't," Alexia replied. "She texts."

"True," Holly agreed, making her way over to the kitchen counter. Instead of Victoria's she saw the name of an editor of a magazine she had recently started to work with. As much as it pained her to take a business call after working hours, it was a relationship she was trying to cultivate.

She answered the call and walked into the hallway so that she wouldn't interrupt Alexia's homework. She tried to maintain a professional conversation, but in the back of her mind she was worried about what Alexia had said.

When Holly moved in with Victoria, she had become a mother to two practically overnight. She loved Hugo and Alexia as if they were her own, but she was also painfully aware that they were not. And she was not a mother who had gained insight and wisdom over the course of many years; she was just some woman who now lived with them. Of course, she hoped they didn't see her like that, but the fear niggled away at her.

What was she? A stepmom? Their mother's girlfriend?

It was all a little muddy.

And being a parent was hard. She was often worried that she'd implement a change that would irreversibly scar one of the children for life.

"Did you get that, Holly?"

She turned her attention back to the phone call. "Yes, sorry, Miriam, I think I lost connection there. I was saying I'd love to take on that article. Can you send over the brief and the deadline to my usual email address? You said you needed it by tomorrow at eleven?"

She sat on the stairs and listened to Miriam talking about the job. Her parenting crisis could wait until after the call.

"Coming through."

She turned. Hugo was coming down the stairs with the

laundry basket in his hands. Holly stood up and walked away from the stairs to allow him past. Every chore in the Hastings household had been carried out by staff when Holly first arrived. Cooking, cleaning, laundry, dog walking. Everything.

Holly had politely explained to Victoria that she wasn't doing her children any favours by having them waited on hand and foot. Now, both children did a few chores to help the staff and to learn how to manage a house.

"All done?" she asked Hugo, her hand over the microphone so Miriam didn't hear.

"Yep. Can I play on my PlayStation now? Or is it nearly dinnertime?"

Holly looked at her watch. Victoria hadn't arrived, nor had she texted to say she'd be late. With the absence of information, Holly decided to go ahead and have dinner on time.

"Nearly dinner, you've got about fifteen minutes."

He nodded and rushed to the laundry room to put the basket away.

She returned her attention to the call. "That's great, Miriam. Thanks for thinking of me. I'll review it tonight, and I'll get the article over to you in the morning."

"Thanks, Holly. I knew I could count on you," Miriam replied, relief evident in her tone.

They said their goodbyes, and Holly hung up.

"New article?" Hugo asked, coming back through the hallway to go upstairs and cram in a few minutes of gaming before dinner.

"Yes, something about conspiracy theorists," she told him.

Hugo took the stairs two at a time. "Flat Earthers?"

"Of course it's flat, Hugo," she deadpanned. "What other shape could it possibly be?"

She heard his laughter from the upper landing and chuckled to herself.

CHAPTER THREE

VICTORIA CLOSED the front door with a small slam.

"Ah, she returns," Holly said as she walked down the stairs towards the entrance hallway. "I didn't expect you for another hour."

"Neither did I," Victoria admitted. "I managed to cut my meeting short due to rampant incompetence. Maybe I should have expected it, considering who the meeting was with."

Holly took her coat and pressed a soft kiss to her cheek. "Well, I'm glad for that incompetence if we get to see you a little sooner. Did you eat?"

Victoria chewed her lip and looked away. There was a rule that she was to eat in the office if she got delayed beyond a certain time. However, she often forgot as time seemed to slip by without permission.

"I'll take that as a no." Holly chuckled as she hung Victoria's coat on the padded hanger in the closet. "Would you like something? I can make you a light salad? Or something more substantial?"

"You don't have to wait on me," Victoria chided her lightly. She was somewhat of an expert at picking foodstuffs out of the fridge for a late-night meal.

"I'm not waiting on you," Holly said. "I'm spending time with you. And this is efficient. You love efficient."

Victoria caught Holly's arm and gently pulled her closer. "I do, but I love you more."

She pressed her lips to Holly's, mindful to keep it light as she desperately wanted to go to the bedroom and freshen up. It had been a long day, and she wanted to get changed, splash some water on her face, and brush her teeth. But Holly was magnetic, and she couldn't go until she'd kissed her.

"Yuck."

Holly pulled away, laughing. Victoria turned towards Hugo, who was coming down the stairs with a wide smirk on his face.

"Would you like to be grounded, Hugo?" Victoria asked sweetly.

"Can you still ground me now that I'm sixteen?" he asked, placing a welcome-home kiss on his mother's cheek.

"We can certainly explore the possibility if you'd like?"

"If anyone's in danger of being grounded, it's you," Hugo told her. "Alexia is unhappy that you're home so late. Again."

Victoria let out a sigh and pinched the bridge of her nose. "It really was unavoidable," she explained softly.

"We know," Holly said. "Go and say hello to her. I'll make you something. What would you like?"

"Is there any tuna left?"

"There is. Tuna salad?" Holly asked.

"That would be lovely." Victoria was already making her way to the stairs, wondering how bad a mood her youngest would be in. Alexia was quite adept at the silent treatment, presumably knowing it was the quickest way to wound Victoria.

"I'll bring it up," Holly said, her tone final.

Victoria's previous rule of no food upstairs had quickly been broken when Holly returned from Paris, and it showed no sign of a resurgence. It felt strange to eat in the living room, but she was aware that it was the best way to maximise her time with her children.

She went to her bedroom first, eagerly stripping out of her waistcoat, trousers, and white blouse. She used the bathroom to freshen up before slipping into a soft, navy sweater and casual, black trousers. She checked her appearance in the mirror before hurrying to the living room.

Alexia's bedtime was eight o'clock. Not five past eight, but eight o'clock on the dot despite many, many arguments to the contrary. Victoria tried her best to maximise her time with Alexia on weekday evenings, but she was painfully aware that she had arrived home at ten minutes to eight once too often in the last week.

She entered the living room. Alexia was lounging on a beanbag watching *Groundhog Day*. Again.

Victoria wondered, not for the first time, what Alexia's fascination with the movie was. Victoria had always thought it was a competent movie, the first time she saw it. Now she could quote the entire thing and wanted it banned from sale in the United States.

"Hello, darling."

Alexia grunted.

Victoria looked at the back of her daughter's head and wondered what the best strategy was.

"I'm sorry I'm late," she tried.

"It's fine," Alexia mumbled, indicating that it wasn't at all fine.

A quick mental scan of her schedule found no gaps she could exploit to make it up to Alexia. It was times like this that she didn't enjoy her prominent role in the publishing world.

She walked around the sofa and the coffee table to the beanbag. She sat cross-legged beside Alexia and looked from her daughter to the large flat screen which held her attention.

"Do you think Holly looks like Andie MacDowell?" Alexia asked.

Victoria looked at the screen and tilted her head to the side. Her overly analytical mind wanted to list all the reasons why Holly looked *nothing* like Andie, but that wasn't going to help her get through to Alexia.

"In some lights," she agreed. "Alexia, I really am—"

"Shh." Alexia gestured towards the television with a nod of her head.

Victoria itched to snatch up the remote control and pause the movie and have a conversation with her daughter. However, she knew that action wouldn't be welcomed. In fact, there was a big chance that would upset Alexia even more than her delayed arrival had.

She needed time to calm down; that's what Holly always

told her, and she was usually correct. Victoria leaned back against the sofa and turned her head to watch the screen. She idly wondered when the fashions would return, as everything eventually did. She didn't look forward to the nineties returning; they were difficult enough the first time around.

An hour later, Victoria returned to the living room from putting Alexia to bed. Holly looked up from her laptop.

"Everything okay?"

"I'm being punished," Victoria explained, fluffing up scatter cushions on her way to the sofa.

"Yes." Holly closed the laptop lid and placed the device on the coffee table. "We need to talk about that."

Victoria let out a sigh. She sat beside Holly. "Must we?"

She didn't feel like being chastised; she'd done her best to get home on time. It wasn't her fault that things were the way they were. There was a deadline that had to be met. Before that there were a set number of meetings and decisions that needed to be finalised. Things overran; it wasn't like she could just leave.

"Unfortunately, yes, but only because of something specific Alexia said," Holly explained.

Victoria's heart sank a little. "Go on…"

"Alexia thinks, or at least said that she thinks, that the only reason you changed your schedule and started to spend more time at home is because of me."

"You?" Victoria frowned.

"Because you wanted to spend more time with me," Holly clarified.

"Well, that's nonsense."

"I know that, and you know that," Holly agreed, "but you must see how it appears to her."

Victoria let out a long sigh, leaned her head back on the sofa, and stared up at the ceiling. "So, I'm damned if I do, damned if I don't."

Holly grabbed her hand and squeezed it. "It's not like that."

"If I stay at work, she'll be angry that I'm not home. If I come home, she'll assume it's to see you." Victoria turned her head and looked at Holly. "Right?"

Holly grinned. "Isn't motherhood great?"

Victoria felt a smile tug at the corner of her mouth.

"This is nothing a conversation won't fix," Holly reassured her.

"Optimist," Victoria whispered. Her eyes were getting heavy, and she knew she'd not be up much longer than her nine-year-old that evening, a depressing thought. "I am sorry."

"For?" Holly asked.

"For being late, for you having to deal with Alexia's moods, for pushing you into the role of motherhood," Victoria started to list the things she felt she had done wrong that evening alone. If they were going to extend the apology to the entire week, then she'd need more time. And a cup of coffee.

Holly discarded her laptop and straddled Victoria's thighs in one swift movement. That woke her up. She lifted her head and looked into determined eyes.

"You have nothing to be sorry for," Holly told her. "I love Alexia and Hugo like they are my own."

"I know you do," Victoria agreed. "But would you really choose to have two children at twenty-six if not for being in a relationship with me?"

"I don't know what I'd choose," Holly admitted, "because it's not worth discussing. This is what I've chosen, to be with you. All of you."

Holly ducked her head down and captured a kiss. It was soft, sweet, and full of promise. Sadly, it only lasted a couple of brief seconds before she sat back up again.

"I had a call about a new job today, an article for *Modern Woman*," Holly said, a satisfied smile on her lips.

She'd earned the smile; she'd been working hard on expanding her profile of late. Holly was a good journalist and article writer, and Victoria was glad to see that she was succeeding at her dream job.

"Wonderful news," Victoria said. "Tight deadline?"

"Yeah, tomorrow before lunch. I've done half of it already. I'm going to sleep on the rest and finish up first thing." Holly ran her finger along the low neck of Victoria's sweater. "Are you very tired?"

Victoria swallowed. She was extremely tired, but she didn't want to turn Holly down.

"I was thinking I could massage you before bed," Holly said.

"Oh. Well, yes, that sounds…" Victoria trailed off. It sounded heavenly. She didn't know what she had done to deserve Holly in her life. The anxiety that it may one day be taken away from her still lingered in the corners of her mind. The ever-present concern that Holly's memories could come back and ruin everything took her breath away when she least expected it.

"What are you thinking about?" Holly asked, immediately picking up on her change in mood.

"Nothing you need to worry about," Victoria replied cryptically.

They'd spoken about Victoria's fears before. The conversation always ended up in a pointless circle. Victoria would state that Holly's memories would one day return and Holly would remember what a vile monster she used to be. Holly would point out that the chances of her memories coming back were slim and growing slimmer each day. She'd then say that it didn't matter if they returned or not; her feelings for Victoria were strong enough to sustain anything.

Victoria wanted to believe that, and she knew that Holly's journals had documented their life together before the accident. She'd never seen them, but she could imagine what young Holly Carter, fresh-faced assistant to ice queen Victoria Hastings, had written in her personal diaries at the start of her employment.

Certainly nothing flattering.

Victoria had been a beast at the start; she always was while breaking in a second assistant. She needed them to be tough if they were going to survive. She could hardly remember a word of what she said to Holly when she worked for her, but she knew she'd probably regret every single utterance.

Holly's detailed journals would surely be nothing compared to the overwhelming sensation of actual memories returning.

"Liar," Holly said. "I can feel you getting more and

more tense by the second." She stood up and reached out her hand. "Come on, let's get you to bed and relax you."

Victoria took Holly's hand and allowed her to be pulled to her feet and led from the sitting room.

Yes, she was indeed a very lucky woman.

CHAPTER FOUR

HOLLY LAY awake in bed and stared at the ceiling. Victoria had fallen asleep during the massage, a sure sign of just how exhausted she was. Luckily, it was only another two days until the issue closed, and then hopefully Victoria's schedule would ease up.

It had been a difficult journey to get Victoria to take a small step back from her work and spend more time with her family.

Holly knew that Victoria was still plagued with nightmares related to Alexia's brief but unexpected misadventure, running away from home the previous year. Initially, Victoria had proclaimed that she'd leave *Arrival* and that her family was far more important than some magazine. She'd quickly climbed down from that view and instead went with the more moderate approach of cutting some of her hours.

Victoria's methodology to problems came in two flavours: a knee-jerk overreaction, or a complete emotional shutdown, complete with retreating into herself and proclaiming that everything was absolutely fine.

Holly had always been good at identifying and managing Victoria's mood swings, if her fastidiously kept journals were anything to go by. Holly could see right through her, and although that may have frustrated Victoria when she was Holly's boss, she seemingly enjoyed reaping the benefits of it now.

Insight into how Victoria worked seemed to be ingrained within her. Even with her memory absent, Holly had quickly been able to identify when Victoria was upset or hiding something. Locating her journals and seeing her past self detailing Victoria's fascinating, yet frustrating, coping mechanisms had been an eye-opening relief.

Having the journals at all had been a relief.

Holly's obsessive habit of documenting every single aspect of her life had been fortuitous to say the least. She'd apparently journaled since she was eight, and she had twenty-nine volumes to show for it.

She believed in fate and that things generally happened for a reason, so when she had found her journal collection in the storage locker a year after the accident, she felt like she had been proved absolutely right.

Obviously, she'd never known that her habit of recording every facet of her life was going to be so important when she'd originally written her diaries. She'd kept some scraps of information written down now and then while she stayed in the hospital in Paris, but nothing much happened, and she had little to say.

Nowadays she dedicated a good hour or two every day to chronicling what was happening. The habit of journaling had taken on a new meaning and depth for her. As much as she tried to stay positive about her brain injury, she'd experienced the shocking situation of quite literally forgetting everything, and she didn't know if it could happen again.

Finding her journals had been a literal lifeline to finding out who she was. Everything had been recorded, often in great detail. Not all of it was easy reading, family deaths, bad breakups, financial strife, and terrible bosses. Well, mainly one terrible boss—Victoria.

Holly still couldn't believe her luck that Victoria had found her in Paris, brought her home, and helped to get her back on her feet. Things could have been so dramatically different for her.

The thought caused a shudder to race up her spine. She turned over in bed and curled her body around Victoria's sleeping form, feeling safe and loved as soon as they touched. She tried to be positive and carefree, but there were times, often at night, when the reality scared her.

While Holly remembered no solid facts before waking up in hospital in Paris twenty-two months ago, she did have feelings of memories. She'd famously remembered Izzy's name, that of Victoria's dog, much to Victoria's disappointment. Not a single memory of Victoria, but the name Izzy sprang to her mind like a light being switched on.

Holly was careful to not get her hopes up, but the fact that she had a sensation of recollection made her think that her memories were in there somewhere, just waiting to come out. Now and then she thought she remembered something, but it was always hazy and more like a half-forgotten dream than an actual memory.

Her doctors had told her the chance of her remembering anything was fifty-fifty, but Holly had quickly ascertained that her doctors knew next to nothing about amnesia. The brain was a wild and complicated series of impulses, and no one seemed to know how or why it did what it did.

Victoria had it in her head that Holly would one day remember. Holly hoped she did but really didn't know if it was possible. Part of Victoria's certainty was rooted in the fact that she still harboured concerns that, if Holly's memories flashed back to life, she'd recall what a difficult woman Victoria had been during her year working with her. The worry was fading over time, but Holly knew it lingered in Victoria's mind. She knew it had been there tonight; she saw it in her eyes.

Not that she could blame her. Holly was keenly aware that her view of their relationship was extremely different from Victoria's. Holly had only had real, tangible memories since she met Victoria in the Paris hospital, a full year after her accident. Everything else was gathered from her journals, knowledge that she had loved Victoria for some time was something she'd only read about. It was documented by her own hand, true and pure, but still distant in some ways. She'd not travelled the path of a conventional relationship and slowly fallen in love over a period of time. She'd been told, by her past self, that the feelings she couldn't quite identify were love. After that, the dam broke, and Holly realised the strength of her emotions.

Victoria had a very different experience. Holly had been an assistant, a second assistant at that. Someone who had gotten closer and closer to Victoria, managing her every need and desire with greater success each week. Victoria, angry at being so predictable to a girl she considered her inferior, rebelled. They were stuck in a battle of Holly doing her best to be the perfect assistant and Victoria doing her best to push her away.

Then, to Victoria's mind, they argued, and Holly walked away. Holly had finally plucked up the courage to admit that she cared for Victoria while in Paris Fashion Week. It was something that Victoria couldn't believe. She thought it a joke, a prank of some kind. She pushed Holly away with acerbic words and a glare that could melt ice.

And then... something. A mystery. An accident of some kind that ripped her life into two distinct pieces. One before Paris, and one after.

Holly held her partner a little tighter, breathing in Victoria's lingering perfume. She knew Victoria had suffered at the thought that Holly had walked away from her. At first she'd felt lost, confused, and angry. A year later, when she found out that Holly had been in an accident, trapped in a hospital in France with amnesia, she'd been horrified and felt immense guilt.

Holly knew that she sometimes underestimated how terrible Victoria still felt about events. The guilt she clearly carried around. Victoria didn't exactly wear her heart on her sleeve. In fact, she did everything she could to hide her feelings most of the time, even from those she loved.

Holly made a mental note to be more considerate of that fact. The truth was, their perception of events was very different. It was a blessing and a curse. Holly didn't know if she wanted to remember the Victoria who had made her cry so many times, and she damn well knew that Victoria didn't want her to remember that.

Still, it was unlikely she would remember. Even now, when memories did resurface, they were like a shadow of the memories themselves. A feeling, rather than an actual memory.

The amnesia hung over their relationship like a dark cloud. While love clearly poured from Victoria onto Holly, there was still a sensation that she was holding something back. It was as if she was not quite one hundred percent in the relationship, trying to protect herself in the eventuality that the worst came to pass. One foot out.

Holly let out a small sigh and tucked her body further against Victoria's, willing herself to succumb to sleep.

CHAPTER FIVE

HOLLY WALKED into the kitchen and greeted Carina with a smile and outstretched, grabby hands for the mug of coffee the housekeeper offered her.

"Life saver," she whispered before taking a sip of the hot beverage.

"Coffee can make your kidneys blow up," Alexia offered in between spoonfuls of cereal.

"Stay in school, sis," Hugo told her as he scrolled on his smartphone.

Holly looked at Alexia sceptically. "Where did you hear that?"

"I saw it online."

"Was it from a credible source?" Holly asked, already knowing the answer was a definite no.

Alexia shrugged and mumbled, "I dunno."

Holly didn't want to nag her first thing in the morning, so she saved the speech about not believing everything found online for another time. She took a seat at the large kitchen table and lifted the lid of her laptop. If she was going to keep to her strict deadline, then she needed to wake up and start working reasonably soon.

"Holly, can I go to Aaron's after school?" Hugo asked.

"Sure, as long as you're home for dinner, and you let your mom know," Holly replied.

Victoria was struggling to identify Hugo as the almost-adult he was. She'd practically missed the fact that he had grown up and often attempted to mother him a little too much. A compromise had been made: Hugo could have more freedom, but he needed to keep Victoria informed of his plans and movements.

"Good morning," Victoria greeted as she walked into the kitchen. "Coffee to go, please, Carina."

"Mom, I'm going to Aaron's after school," Hugo announced without looking up from his phone.

Holly reached out with her foot and gave him a soft kick. He looked up at her in confusion for a couple of moments before realisation dawned. He turned to face his mother.

"I mean, I just asked Holly, and she said it was okay. And I'll be home for dinner," he added.

Carina handed Victoria a stainless-steel travel mug as Victoria looked at Hugo, a slight pursing of her lips clear. Holly watched and waited to see what happened next.

"Very well. Don't be late," she finally said.

Holly let out a soft sigh of relief. There had been a couple of arguments between mother and son as they vied for dominance. It was nice to see things settling down.

"Mom, can we watch *Toy Story* this weekend?" Alexia asked.

Holly stifled a chuckle and returned her attention to her

laptop. When they had spoken the night before, Victoria had stated that she would 'do whatever it took' to spend more time with her daughter and ensure she wasn't feeling left out. Watching the children's movie for the eighteenth time that year was probably not something she envisaged as part of that plan.

"Well, we could," Victoria said, her voice soft and placating. "But maybe we could do something else? We could go shopping."

"Mom, you know I don't like shopping," Alexia pointed out. "You like shopping, remember? I'm the person who finds shopping mega boring."

Holly tuned out of the conversation, her attention distracted by a mysterious email in her inbox. She didn't recognise the sender's name, but the subject line stated it was urgent and the contents has been marked as private and confidential.

Confident in her virus protection software, she opened the email. The breath left her lungs, and her skin instantly felt ice cold. Picture after picture loaded in the body of the email, and she was thankful that her screen was obscured from anyone else.

Her hand shook as she traced her finger over the trackpad and scrolled down the email. Her lungs began to burn. She reminded herself to breathe, darting a quick glance around the table to check that everyone was still occupied and not paying her any attention.

Satisfied that her panic had gone unnoticed, she looked back to the email and the photographs of Victoria with another woman. More specifically, kissing another woman.

There were six images in total; four showed Victoria

walking or talking with the mystery woman down a street that appeared to be in New York. Two of the images showed the pair in an intimate embrace and kissing in a definitely sexual manner.

This can't be right, Holly thought. *It can't be. Maybe this is from ages ago?*

She tilted her head as she regarded the other woman; she zoomed in a little and realised she recognised her. It was Ashley Somerset. Holly had been introduced to her by Victoria a couple of months before at an *Arrival* event. Holly searched her memory and recalled that Ashley was something in the art studio. More importantly, Ashley was new to *Arrival*. Victoria had explained how she had poached her from *Arrival London,* which meant these photographs couldn't be from years ago. They were recent. As in, they had been taken since Victoria and Holly had been together.

Holly's hand started to shake even more. She snatched it away from the trackpad and held it in her other hand under the table.

She stared at the picture, thinking that there was something obvious she was missing. Maybe it wasn't Victoria? Or perhaps it wasn't recent after all. But if that was the case, then why hadn't Victoria mentioned a history with Ashley?

There had to be something obvious that she wasn't seeing, but she couldn't think straight as long as the images taunted her.

"Holly?"

She snapped her eyes up to meet Alexia's. "Sorry, sweetie, what did you say?"

"Do you want to come to the zoo this weekend with me and Mom?"

Holly's gaze drifted to Victoria, who was looking at her with mild concern. She had presumably detected that something was wrong but not wanted to bring attention to it.

"I... don't know," Holly admitted. Suddenly, she didn't know anything at all. "I might be working. We'll see, okay?"

Alexia nodded, happy enough with the vague answer. She picked up her bowl and walked over to Carina, thanking her for breakfast before leaving the kitchen to finish getting ready.

"Is everything okay?" Victoria asked.

Holly couldn't answer that. No, nothing was okay, but she didn't want to say anything in front of Carina and Hugo. Not that she felt strong enough to say anything anyway. She felt for sure that her heart would break in two if she so much as looked at the images on her laptop screen again.

She softly closed the lid.

"Fine," she lied. "Just distracted. Work."

She knew she was a terrible liar, hated that she was lying in the first place, but she didn't know what else to do.

"Are you sure?" Victoria asked, cutting right through her flimsy subterfuge.

Holly quickly nodded her head. She stood up, eager to get out of the line of questioning. "I'm going to make sure Alexia remembers her homework," she lied. "I'll talk to you later."

She all but ran from the kitchen, hoping that Victoria wouldn't follow her.

CHAPTER SIX

GIDEON TAPPED the top of his mechanical pencil, expecting a little more lead to show itself. Nothing happened. He pressed the button a few more times before realising it was time to refill.

It was a mark of how busy he was. He'd only refilled the pencil a week before. He opened his desk drawer and took out a box of Faber-Castell leads and started to replenish the pencil.

In the distance he heard a very determined pair of heels clacking down the hallway. He knew there was a fifty percent chance that Victoria would bypass his office and head straight into the art department.

He felt the breeze of his office door opening. It seemed that luck wasn't on his side.

He pointed to the empty stool in the corner of his office without saying a word. He heard Victoria sit down, and a few moments later she exhaled deeply.

He finished what he was doing, put the box of leads

away, placed his pencil on its stand, and then turned to regard Victoria.

"Good morning," he greeted her with a smile.

"Holly's having an affair." Victoria gazed at the tip of her shoe with disinterest.

"I'd be very surprised if that were true," he replied neutrally.

"It was bound to happen eventually. She's young and has her whole life in front of her," Victoria said casually. "I thought I'd let you know, before the media does."

Gideon didn't believe for a second that Holly would have an affair. He'd spoken to her just the other week, and the girl was as sickly in love as she had been since she'd first gotten together with Victoria. Not to mention he was very used to Victoria's habit of making mountains out of molehills.

"Must be a recent thing," he commented. "She was telling me just last week how wonderful you allegedly are. Can't see it myself."

"This isn't a laughing matter." Victoria looked up; anger flashed in her eyes.

To Gideon, the whole thing was ridiculous, but he knew that Victoria had a very different mindset to him. She'd gathered up information and extrapolated the craziest explanation, but to her, it was real. He had to respect that, while also trying to get her to reason.

"No, of course. So, who is she having this affair with? When is she moving out? Or has she already moved out?" Gideon questioned.

He knew that Holly wouldn't have moved out; the very

thought was impossible to believe. Victoria had jumped the gun, and he wanted her to see that.

"Obviously I don't know all the sordid details," Victoria argued. She looked away again, examining the awards that hung on the wall.

"What do you know?" he fished.

"She's hiding something." Victoria slowly turned her head, meeting Gideon with a self-assured look.

"Aren't we all?"

"There was very clearly something on her mind this morning. She all but ran out on breakfast, but she refused to admit something was wrong."

"Maybe it was something that you don't need to know about? Maybe she felt ill?"

"Well, possibly," Victoria allowed. She turned a little green at the very thought of someone vomiting, a peculiar Achilles heel of hers.

"Or maybe she was just tired?"

"Well, yes, of course that's a possibility. But let's look at the facts here, Gideon—"

He chuckled and folded his arms. "Yes, please let's look at these facts. Do you have any?"

She slid off the stool. "I don't know why I confide in you. This warped sense of humour isn't charming, Gideon."

She'd stood up but clearly had no intention of leaving. She wanted to hear his advice but wasn't about to ask for it. Classic Victoria Hastings.

"Holly adores you," Gideon told her. "She's hopelessly in love with you. While you may be convinced that she will one day fall out of love with you, I will eat the next issue of *Arrival* if that happened this morning over breakfast."

"I'm not convinced of any such thing," Victoria denied.

"Hmm." Gideon sat down and picked up his pencil. He started to sketch the layout he was envisaging for the winter wonderland spread. He could feel Victoria staring at him, waiting for him to say something else.

"Well?" she finally asked, irritated at his continued silent treatment and lack of advice.

"Holly isn't having an affair, and if you think she is, then you should really be talking to her and not me about it. Just don't do anything rash, Victoria."

"When have you *ever* known me to act rashly?" she complained. "I really don't know why I talk to you about these things. What kind of advice is that? Oh, and I'm pushing up the editorial meeting to two o'clock. And please don't try to pitch anything that requires a snow machine for the winter spread. The way climate change is going, we'll all be associating snow with summer by the time the issue goes out. Think beach balls rather than polar bears, mark my words."

He felt the breeze of air as his office door opened and closed again. He heard heels clicking into the distance, this time sounding less determined and a little more relaxed.

He grinned to himself and shook his head.

CHAPTER SEVEN

HOLLY TOYED with her empty tea cup, slowly running her
finger along the edge of it. Her gaze was fixed on the
multiple doors to the *Arrival* office across the busy street. If
she had Victoria's schedule right, and she usually did, then
Victoria would be leaving the building shortly for a meeting
across town.

She hated what she was about to do, but felt it was
necessary because she needed answers. She hated how she
had acted around Victoria that morning. Being tired,
confused, and hurt meant not being able to be as bright and
happy as she usually was before Victoria left for work.

As soon as Victoria had left for work with a slam of the
front door, Holly had regretted not speaking to her there
and then. She tried to justify it to herself by claiming that
Victoria was busy and didn't have time to discuss the matter
before a busy day at *Arrival*.

The truth was that she was scared, frightened that she'd
been naïve and living a lie, even though the very idea
seemed absolutely absurd to her. If she wasn't going to speak

to Victoria directly, then she needed to find answers some other way. Even if she knew it meant sneaking around behind Victoria's back to get them.

The object of her thoughts walked out of the *Arrival* office, dark sunglasses firmly in place and her first assistant, Louise, barely able to keep up with her long strides. Within a matter of seconds, they were both in the Town Car and on their way to their meeting.

Holly knew she had about an hour to do what she needed to do. Not that she was entirely sure what that was yet. Her plan was half-formed at best.

She grabbed her bag and hurried from the coffee shop. A fortuitous gap in traffic meant she could cross the road immediately. She put her hand in her pocket and wrapped it around the permanent *Arrival* visitor pass she had. She may no longer have been a member of staff, but she still had access to the office whenever she wanted it. Access she was about to use for less than honest reasons.

"Afternoon, Miss Carter," Bobby, the security guard, greeted her warmly.

"Hello, Bobby," she replied with a smile.

"You just missed her," he said apologetically.

"I know, I'm planning a surprise," she explained with a wink.

"Ah!" He nodded knowingly and returned the wink.

She passed through the turnstiles and got into an elevator, selecting the top floor of the *Arrival* offices. Her heart was pounding in her chest, and her palms were sweaty. She hoped she didn't look too suspicious. Holly just wasn't made for deception. She was inherently honest. As far as she was concerned, there was nothing that couldn't be resolved by a conversation over a hot drink.

Except this. This was bigger than that. This was potentially the end of her happy life with Victoria, even if she couldn't believe it. Her heart kept telling her why it was impossible, only for her brain to display an image of Victoria in a passionate embrace with someone else.

The elevator doors opened. She quickly stepped out and made her way towards the large corner office dedicated to the editor-in-chief. Claudia sat in the outer office, typing.

"Hi Holly!"

"Hi." Holly held the shoulder strap of her bag tightly.

"Victoria's not here." Claudia looked apologetic.

"Oh, yes, I forgot. She has that meeting." Holly bit her lip thoughtfully. "It's fine, I was just passing anyway. Say, I'm writing an article, and it would be super helpful if I could speak to someone in the art studio. What floor is it on?"

"This one," Claudia said brightly. "Literally down that corridor to the very end and then turn right."

"That's great. Thanks, Claudia. Oh, and don't let Victoria know I was here. She'll never let me forget that I don't pay attention when she's telling me about her schedule." She laughed.

"No problem, we're not exactly buddies anyway." Claudia's phone rang. "Back to the grindstone," she whispered before answering the call.

Holly sucked in a deep breath and walked down the long corridor to the other end of the building, doing her best to smile at people who greeted her as she walked. Some of them knew her from when she worked there; some of them just knew her as Victoria's partner. In any event, she had to keep a smile on her face despite the thundering of her heart against her ribcage.

She looked into Gideon's office as she passed, her heart sinking when she found it empty. He'd have answers for her; there was nothing at *Arrival* that he didn't know about. She'd call him later, once she'd spoken with Ashley.

Her heart was beating faster and harder as she closed in on the art studio. She still wasn't entirely sure what she was going to say to Ashley when she saw her. She was hoping that the tall, long-haired blonde's face would tell her everything she needed to know. Surely being confronted by Holly would be enough for her to know she'd been rumbled?

Holly entered the art department and approached the receptionist.

"Hi, is Ashley in?" she asked.

"Hi, Holly. Yes, she's at her desk, you can go right in." The receptionist pointed towards a bank of desks. Holly's eye immediately found Ashley. She gave the receptionist a nod and walked towards the other woman, still not entirely sure what was about to happen.

"Oh, hi!" Ashley greeted her the moment she saw Holly.

Holly tried to return the bright smile but struggled. Ashley seemed genuinely happy to see her and without a single trace of fear or apprehension about Holly's unusual presence in the art studio.

"Hi, Ashley," she said. "I need to talk to you."

"Sure, let me grab you a seat." Ashley jumped up and brushed past Holly to get a spare office chair. She wheeled it over to the edge of her desk and gestured for Holly to sit down. "Can I get you a drink?"

Holly sat down, confused. This wasn't the welcome she'd expected at all. She'd pictured Ashley blushing, running away, crying, begging forgiveness, or just denying everything before Holly said a word. A warm welcome and the offer of a drink hadn't occurred to her at all.

"Tea? Coffee?" Ashley suggested at the prolonged silence. "Oh, by the way, I read your piece in the *New York Lifestyle* last month. You are so right about travelling versus ecological awareness. I feel that subject very deeply, especially with all my family being in England. Every time I fly home to see them, I feel like I'm personally poking a hole in the ozone layer."

Something was wrong. Very, very wrong. There was no way that Ashley was this good of an actress.

"Yes, it's a real issue," Holly agreed, realising that she needed to break her silence.

"And then you use technology, but are those companies telling the truth about their green credentials? How do I know that my voice app provider isn't pumping out enough CO_2 to match my plane and then some?" Ashley shook her head. "Anyway, I'm sorry. You wanted to talk to me? Oh, and did you want a drink?"

Holly stepped into the elevator and stabbed the ground floor button. She was even more confused now than when she'd arrived. Her brain was swimming with questions and half-baked theories.

The elevator bounced to a gentle stop almost immediately after starting its downward journey. The doors opened, and a man stepped in. He was in his forties, ruggedly attractive, and very well dressed.

"Holly Carter," he announced with a smile. "So good to see you again. I heard you were back."

Here we go, Holly thought, mentally preparing to go into her speech about her accident and her memory loss.

He selected a floor on the elevator panel and then turned back to face her as the doors slid closed. "Victoria told me about your memory, so I assume you don't remember me?"

"Um. No…" Holly was stunned. It wasn't like Victoria to explain anything. To anyone. Ever.

"I'm Steven Goodfellow." He held out his hand.

Holly shook it. Victoria had mentioned him, but she was so shaken up, she couldn't quite remember where or when.

"Is Victoria treating you well?" he asked, obviously aware of their relationship.

"She is," Holly confirmed, not sure if that was entirely true or not. All she wanted to do now was get out of the elevator, out of the *Arrival* offices, to somewhere she could take a breath and think.

"Victoria invited me to dinner, but I'm so swamped with things at the moment. Please tell her that I'll get back to her as soon as I can. I'd love to catch up with you both."

"I'll definitely pass that on," Holly agreed.

"Love the new hair," he said, pointing to her short cut.

"Thank you."

The elevator doors opened, and he smiled amiably

before stepping out. She tried her best to return the smile but was pretty sure she failed miserably. The doors closed and she slumped against the wall of the elevator cart, trying her best to hold back the tears that were threatening to spill down her cheeks.

CHAPTER EIGHT

VICTORIA OPENED the front door and immediately heard the sound of Alexia running down the stairs from the sitting room.

"Hey, Mom!"

She let out a sigh of relief. That was the greeting she wanted when she got home. Not the silent treatment of the previous evening. Of course, it was a hard-fought victory that had meant leaving the office early despite the deadlines that were piling up.

But her daughter came first. Alexia launched herself into Victoria, wrapping her arms around her middle. Victoria held her tightly and let a small, satisfied smile curl at her lips. It was a rare occurrence that her daughter was so exceptionally happy to see her, one that grew rarer each year.

"Hello, darling," she greeted.

"Carina made lasagne, but she used low-fat cheese," Alexia explained.

"Carina?" Victoria questioned. "I thought Holly was cooking this evening."

Holly had been experimenting with various hobbies she used to partake in, trying to rediscover her interests. She had never had much time for cooking before, her ex being a professional chef who had constantly taken control of the kitchen. After moving in with Victoria, Holly had happily started trying her hand at various meals and before long found that she enjoyed it very much. Stress relief, she'd claimed.

"Holly isn't here," Alexia explained. She took a step back and opened up the hallway closet, pulling out a padded hanger for Victoria's coat.

Victoria placed her bag on the telephone table and shrugged out of her coat. Holly was always home before her, and if she wasn't, then she always called or at least sent a text. Now that she was thinking about it, she hadn't heard from Holly at all that day.

Victoria usually sent a text message or two throughout the course of the day, but she hadn't thought to do so. Her mind still swam with Holly's obvious upset from the morning. She'd convinced herself she was giving Holly space, but maybe she'd just been afraid of whatever was lurking in the dark spaces in Holly's eyes that morning.

"Where is she?" she asked, taking the proffered hanger and putting her coat away.

Alexia shrugged. "I dunno."

"'Dunno' is not a word in this house," Victoria said. The appalling slang was fast becoming Alexia's go-to answer for everything.

"It's a word according to Merriam-Webster," Alexia defended herself.

Victoria closed the closet door. "You'll look that up, but

checking the source of a news story that claims that manatees could play the piano if given the chance escapes you?"

"They have an amazing sense of musicality," Alexia explained.

Victoria got her phone out of her bag. She had no messages waiting for her, so she quickly fired off a text message to Holly asking where she was and when she'd be home.

"I need to speak to Carina; I'll meet you upstairs in a moment," Victoria said. The question of the musical ability of sea mammals would have to wait.

Alexia knew when she was being dismissed and climbed the stairs, two at a time, calling out to her brother that their mother was home.

Victoria entered the kitchen where Carina was busy washing up. "I hear we're having lasagne tonight?"

Carina looked up and smiled. "Yes, with the low-fat cheese. I made extra salad, too."

"Excellent, thank you." Victoria's own diet was bland and rarely contained any such treats as cheese, or any unnecessary fats or sugars, but she knew that her children didn't enjoy such a boring selection. A compromise was found, the occasional 'bad' meal but with plenty of healthy sides. Balance.

"Has Holly been in touch?" Victoria asked casually, not wanting to admit to her housekeeper that she'd not heard from her girlfriend.

"Only to ask me to stay this afternoon to watch the children and to prepare dinner. She said something had come up and she wouldn't be back in time."

"Did she say when she would be back?"

Carina shook her head. "Sorry, no."

Victoria looked at her phone again, hoping for a reply.

Her screensaver, a happy family scene in the local park, looked back at her mockingly. She gripped the device tightly and stalked towards her office, not willing to allow Carina to see her amidst yet another relationship struggle.

Carina had been her housekeeper for almost twenty years. She'd seen it all before, but Victoria hoped that this would be different. She'd almost managed to convince herself that her unconventional relationship with Holly was different, but it seemed it had the ability to be just as dysfunctional as what had gone before. Somehow, Holly was upset and missing.

No note. No text. Nothing. Holly was just… gone.

She felt a sudden chill. Holly's strange mood that morning and now her disappearance. Maybe her overreaction in Gideon's office wasn't so off base after all. Perhaps Holly was having an affair. Or maybe her memories had returned?

Victoria reached for the wall to steady herself.

Was everything about to fall apart?

"You're being ridiculous," she told herself. "Just wait until she gets home and then talk to her. Like she always says, there's nothing that can't be solved by communication."

She sagged into her office chair, not quite believing the words but hoping against hope that they were true. She looked at her mobile phone again.

Still nothing.

CHAPTER NINE

HOLLY HURRIED up the steps to the townhouse she shared with Victoria. She unlocked the door and entered the house, hoping that she had arrived late enough that the children were in bed and asleep.

Victoria appeared from the kitchen, her eyes wild and her cheeks red from tears. Holly didn't stop to answer any questions and threw herself into Victoria's arms.

"I'm sorry," she whispered.

"Where have you been?" Victoria spluttered. "Why didn't you answer your phone?"

Holly leaned back, cupped Victoria's head in her hands, and kissed her with as much feeling as she could impart. What she was about to tell Victoria would break her into pieces, the least she could do was try to soften the blow.

Victoria fell into the kiss, eagerly wrapping her arms around Holly and holding her tightly. Minutes went by, filled with passionate kisses and soft apologies. Eventually Holly leaned back in Victoria's arms so she could speak.

"We have to talk," she said.

"What's going on?" Victoria demanded in a cross, though hushed, tone. "You know I hate being out of the loop. I thought something had happened to you. I was about to call the police!"

Holly brushed Victoria's locks away from her face. "I know, I'm sorry. I've had a really long day looking into things. Can we go to your office and talk?"

Victoria looked uncertain, almost afraid. Holly couldn't blame her. She nodded and slowly released Holly from her grip.

"Are the kids asleep?" Holly asked as they entered the office. She closed the door.

"Yes, I told them you were working on an article and had an interview to go to this evening. Not that I *enjoy* lying to them."

"I know," Holly said. "I'm sorry I put you in that position."

"Tell me what's happening," Victoria demanded. Her arms were folded and her gaze severe, but Holly could see through the Hastings bluster and knew that Victoria was terrified. Now Holly needed to explain everything.

Holly sat on the sofa and pulled her MacBook out of her satchel. She patted the place beside her and opened the lid.

"I got an email this morning," she explained, "which was why I acted strangely over breakfast. I should have spoken to you then, but, well, I was in shock."

Victoria perched on the sofa beside her, seemingly unwilling to sit comfortably. Holly knew that was only going to get worse as she explained what had happened that day. She opened the original email and turned her laptop around to face Victoria.

She watched as Victoria blinked, then leaned in, then sat back in shock. A second later she was leaning in again, staring in abject confusion at what was on the screen.

"What…" Victoria gasped. Her eyes shot up to meet Holly's. "This is—"

"Fake. I know," Holly said. "I *didn't* know that this morning."

"I'd never…" Victoria leaned closer to the screen again. "Is that Ashley Somerset?"

"Yes."

"This is… it's… ludicrous. I'd never. I'm not and would never," Victoria stammered.

"I know. At first, I didn't know what to think," Holly confessed. "I went to *Arrival* today, to speak to Ashley and see what she had to say."

"She'll tell you the same as I told you," Victoria said with absolute certainty.

"She didn't have to. The moment I started speaking to her, I knew nothing was going on between you. I pretended I had some questions for an article I was writing. We had tea and chatted for a while." Holly ran a hand through her hair. Her emotions had been dragged through the wringer all day. Shock, confusion, anger, more confusion, realisation, and then far more anger.

"I got another email this afternoon," she continued. She didn't move for a moment, wanting to settle herself before having to see the crass image again.

"Dare I ask?" Victoria asked, prompting her into action.

Holly sucked in a breath and turned the laptop to face

her. She clicked a few buttons and then averted her eyes as she turned the screen towards Victoria.

"Oh my," Victoria breathed.

Holly saw that she was far less embarrassed at viewing the image than Holly had been. Presumably this had something to do with her job and seeing women in various states of undress during photoshoots.

"Well..." Victoria swallowed. "This is fabrication."

Holly closed the lid of the laptop and put it to one side. It may have been a fake image, but seeing Victoria in bed with another woman had still broken Holly's heart.

Victoria reached out and took her hand. "I assure you—"

"You don't need to," Holly said. "I know both images are fakes, but they are very good fakes. I took them to someone I know, a professional. She said that less than twenty percent of forensic photograph examiners would be able to tell that these were fake. They are *that* good."

"But you know, right?" Victoria asked, gripping Holly's hand. "You know these are nonsensical fabrications?"

"I do," Holly confirmed. She squeezed Victoria's hand. "But you know what this means, don't you?"

Victoria slowly nodded. "I'm going to murder whoever sent you those images."

"Victoria, these are incredibly sophisticated fakes," Holly pointed out, hoping that she would soon catch up.

"Do I congratulate the fraudster?" Victoria demanded, her voice ever so slightly raised. This was concerning because Holly had only ever heard Victoria shout three times the entire time she'd known her. "Tell me, is it more appropriate to send chocolates or flowers?"

"Victoria, listen to me," Holly snapped. She pulled her hand away. She needed Victoria to see the situation for what it was. "This is serious."

Victoria swallowed down her next sarcastic comment and looked at Holly. "Then we hire someone to investigate," she said. "Or we wait for the email that will no doubt arrive by the morning requesting money."

"There's something else," Holly said.

Victoria's eyes widened. "More?"

Holly opened her laptop, quickly closing down the photograph of Ashley and Victoria in a naked embrace. Her fingers danced across the trackpad to the latest email. She took a deep breath and opened it.

She angled the screen towards Victoria and watched as the older woman read the contents.

There were no images in the third and final email. It was just text, text that Holly had memorised. It claimed that the sender was a friend, someone who wanted the best for Holly. It went on to claim that, on top of Victoria's affair, the editor-in-chief had another secret.

It claimed that the power of attorney Victoria had briefly held over Holly in order to be able to get her home, the one that had been annulled as soon as they started dating, was still in force.

"What?" Victoria asked, before shaking her head and reading the email again.

"It claims that you didn't annul the power of attorney," Holly explained. "It's saying that you still have legal control over me. And it's saying I should be careful. Of you."

"That's absolutely preposterous," Victoria announced. "Who is this imbecile?"

Holly had asked herself that question a hundred times. She had no idea who would send her such emails, no idea who would spend so much time creating such sophisticated images.

But she did know one thing.

Whoever it was was desperate to pull them apart and seemingly had no scruples about how that was achieved.

"I don't know," Holly admitted, "but very few people ever knew about the power of attorney. If that gets out to the public, just think what people will say."

Their relationship had already caused eyebrows to be raised. Talk of the impropriety of Victoria dating a former assistant who was almost half her age raged on in the gossip columns. If the paparazzi knew about the power of attorney, Holly could only imagine the reaction.

"I don't care what people say." Victoria jutted her chin out defiantly.

"You should," Holly said. She may not have been a journalist long, but she already knew how easy it was for a news story to destroy lives. For all of Victoria's bravado, Holly knew that she feared bad press just as much as anyone else. Opinion was easily swayed, and often the rolling ball of gutter journalism was unstoppable.

Victoria blinked. "So, what do you suggest?"

Holly sucked in a deep breath. Victoria wasn't going to like what she was about to say. Not one bit.

"This isn't a simple prank, honey. This is bigger than that. Someone has been sending me these emails very deliberately. They've set a series of events in motion, and I intend to follow them. It's the only way to figure out who is doing this and why."

Victoria frowned. "What do you mean, you intend on following this series of events?"

Holly knew it was the moment to explain her plan in all of its terrible detail. She sucked in a quick breath. "I… I'm moving out."

"What?!" Victoria yelled.

Four times, Holly thought to herself.

"No, absolutely not. This… this is utter madness. How has this even *happened*?" Victoria jumped up and paced her office. "We were happy just a few hours ago."

"We are happy," Holly reassured her partner. She stood in front of Victoria and softly took her face in her hands. "We *are* happy. But someone is setting you up and they seem determined to separate us."

"So, you're letting them?" Victoria was starting to calm down as Holly gently caressed her cheeks with her thumbs, confusion and fear replacing the outrage.

"No, I'm giving them the *impression* that they have. Think about it. If this doesn't work, what will they do next? What's the encore? I don't want to see you get hurt, I don't want someone messing with our family."

Holly lowered her hands; she took Victoria's in hers and leaned forward to try to catch her gaze. The older woman looked steadfastly at the ground, refusing to make eye contact.

"I don't want to do this," Victoria whispered.

Holly felt her heart break. Victoria was always the strong one. Seeing her so despondent was a bitter pill to swallow.

"I don't want to," she repeated.

"I don't want to either," Holly agreed. "But we have to

do this. Whoever is doing this knows that I received these emails. Right now, I can do one of two things: believe the emails or realise they are fake."

"And you know they are fake," Victoria said, her tear-filled eyes meeting Holly's.

"I do, but I don't want them to know that. I want them to be confident that it worked, maybe a little cocky. It will make it easier to find them. Victoria, this person wants to break us up. Why?"

"How should I know the scheming mind of a derange—"

"Exactly. And that frightens me," Holly admitted. "If we play the game, make it look like I'm here this evening to have it out with you and finish things, then we can investigate without arousing suspicions."

"Don't move out tonight. Go on the weekend… or tomorrow… but not tonight," Victoria pleaded.

Holly sucked in a deep breath and shakily let it out. "I… I already have a hotel. I packed some things and took them there before the kids got home."

Victoria paled, and Holly wondered if she might faint. She tightened her grip on Victoria's hands.

"But it's not real," Holly reassured. "We're going to beat this. Together."

CHAPTER TEN

VICTORIA FELT as though the room was spinning out of control. How had it come to this, from a completely typical workday to her home life falling down around her ears? It didn't make any sense.

"We can hire security," she decided. "There's no need for you to leave. I'll get the best. We can even employ hackers, just tell me where to find them."

She looked into Holly's sympathetic eyes, upset with herself for crying and causing her vision to become a blurred mess.

Holly gently shook her head. "I'm sorry. I'm worried it won't work, that we won't be able to figure out who it is before they do something else. I want to know who this person is, Victoria. I want to know what their plan is."

"Do we really care about this… this… madman?" Victoria asked.

"I do," Holly admitted. "They are trying to separate us. They are trying to frame you. And what if…" She took a deep breath. "Long shot, but what if they know something about my accident? They know about the power of attorney, which so very few people know about. Maybe they know something else?"

Victoria's swirling thoughts stopped dead in their tracks. She'd never been one to care about rumours directed at herself. If she'd worried about false newspaper reports, then she would have left *Arrival* years ago. Not a day went by when a new, often fictitious story about her was broadcast to the world.

But this wasn't just her; this included Holly. Someone was targeting them both. Holly had a right to be involved in deciding what they did next, even if Victoria really hated the plan that Holly had apparently already chosen. She wished she hadn't set her plan in stone before they even had a chance to discuss it.

"Can't we discuss this?" Victoria asked.

Holly looked apologetic. "I know you want me to stay. I want to stay, believe me, I do. But I get the feeling that someone is watching us, waiting to see how we'll react."

Victoria threw up her hands in resignation and crossed the room. She leaned against her desk and stared down at her shoes. There didn't seem to be a way out of whatever was happening to them.

They didn't have any information on who was involved or what they wanted. There was a possibility that a demand for money would arrive, but it wasn't assured. This didn't seem to be the usual scam; it felt bigger than that.

Which was exactly why Holly was suggesting her plan.

"So, what—exactly—do you recommend we do?"

Victoria wasn't agreeing to anything just yet. She wanted to hear what Holly had in mind. Not that she really thought she had any say in the matter. Holly was steadfast and determined when she had an idea.

"When I leave tonight, I'll go to my hotel. Tomorrow, we'll start telling people that we've had an argument and I've moved out. Well, I'll tell people that. You need to act like you normally would," Holly explained.

Victoria blinked. "And how do I *normally act*?" she questioned.

"Aloof," Holly said without a hesitation. "It's not like you hang out around the water cooler discussing your life. So, you just act as you normally would. Maybe spill the beans to Gideon, maybe loud enough for Louise and Claudia to overhear. Or drop a sarcastic comment somewhere public as you frequently do."

"Aloof? Sarcastic comment?" Victoria asked petulantly. "Is that how you see me?"

Holly sighed. "No, that's not how I see you. But it is how you act at work, and don't you deny it."

Victoria found herself trapped between knowing full well that was how she acted and being frustrated at being called out on it. She decided to remain silent.

"Then we need to see who starts acting strangely," Holly said.

"And how, pray tell, do we do that?"

Holly walked over, took Victoria's hands again, and looked her in the eye. "We see if someone is fishing for information, if someone seems to be acting out of the ordinary," she explained. "And we'll need a list."

"A list?"

"Of suspects. Louise is definitely on that list," Holly said.

"Louise?" Victoria frowned. Her first assistant hadn't done anything to warrant being placed at the top of Holly's list. Not to her knowledge. "Why Louise?"

"She's snooty, rude, has always hated me, and often used to play pranks to ensure I got into trouble with you," Holly explained.

Victoria blinked. "You never said anything."

"It's in the past," Holly stated. "She either has a massive crush on you, or she hero-worships you. Either way she doesn't like me, and I wouldn't put anything past her."

"Well then, I petition we put Samuel on the list. He's scruffy. I never trust anyone scruffy," Victoria said. She also didn't like how the French reporter had stayed in contact with Holly, not that she'd said anything about it directly.

"Fine, Sam can be on the list if you insist. But for the record I think we can trust him," Holly argued.

"His eyes are far too close together. It's amazing he doesn't constantly trip over."

"Now you're being ridiculous." Holly let go of her hands, and Victoria immediately felt the loss. "Lucy from *Arrival* accounts hates you. And she's very technically savvy."

"If we're going to add anyone who hates me to this list, then I fear we must add all *Arrival* staff," Victoria suggested sarcastically.

"Actually, I think that's true. In fact, I think we should work to eliminate people from our enquiries rather than the other way around."

"So… all of *Arrival* goes on the list?" Victoria clarified.

"Yes." Holly nodded. She scrunched up her face and looked thoughtfully at the ceiling. Victoria watched, intrigued by this detective version of her girlfriend who stood before her.

Sweet Holly who didn't have a bad word to say about anyone suddenly didn't trust a single person. Except Victoria, despite the apparent evidence to the contrary. She felt her heart swell at that knowledge.

"Yes, we'll consider everyone a suspect at the moment and then rank them or eliminate them based on their behaviour. At the moment, you, me, and the kids are the only people…"

Their eyes met in concern.

"The children," Victoria whispered. She hadn't even considered that aspect right up until that very moment.

"I'll take the blame," Holly immediately said. "I'll tell them that I did something wrong. We don't need to give too many details."

"Absolutely not." Victoria shook her head and pushed herself up from her desk to stand her ground. "No. They adore you. I won't have you taking the fall for this."

"They're already quick enough to blame you for everything," Holly replied.

It was true, but it was also warranted. Victoria had spent most of her children's lives being the one who disappointed them, the one who came home late, the one who cancelled holidays and outings. Victoria was used to being the bad guy in the house. She wasn't about to have Holly's reputation sullied for no reason.

She shrugged. "They'll assume it's my fault anyway."

"Well, I'll convince them otherwise," Holly said.

"What will you say?" Victoria asked. "What will we both say? To everyone?" She rubbed her forehead. The whole situation was exhausting her. All she wanted to do was crawl into bed with her girlfriend and forget the whole thing, but she knew that wasn't in the cards. "And where are you going?"

"To a hotel," Holly answered simply.

"Which one? Please tell me it's not some horrible motel. Let me call Sebastian and get you a room at—"

"Victoria, you can't be involved. It has to appear as if I'm *leaving you*, not that you called your travel agent and arranged a luxury midweek stay for me. I'm staying in a nice hotel, don't worry."

Victoria narrowed her eyes. "Which hotel?"

Holly pursed her lips and refused to make eye contact.

"You won't tell me?" Victoria couldn't believe it.

"I know you. You'll worry and you'll send food. Or clothes. Books. You'll even turn up to inspect it," Holly said. "We have to act as if I've… as if I've left."

Victoria opened her mouth, willing herself to issue the denial, but she knew it was true. If she knew the hotel, then she would turn up unannounced. She'd ensure that the manager knew exactly what precious cargo they had slumbering in one of their rooms.

Damn Holly for knowing her so well and for always being one step ahead of her.

Holly crossed the room and pulled Victoria into a hug. She quickly wrapped her arms around the younger woman, wondering when they'd be able to do such a thing again.

"I will figure this out, I promise," Holly said. "And I'll be in touch. We'll need to meet up to discuss what we have found out."

"Why would anyone want us apart?" Victoria wondered aloud.

"Well, remember I'm a gold digger," Holly joked, referencing Victoria's sister's comments.

"Oh, yes, and I'm a cradle robber," Victoria replied, remembering Holly's ex-girlfriend's less than kind comments.

Holly adjusted her head to lay atop Victoria's shoulder. "If it was just that, I'd ignore it, but this is much worse. This is creating authentic-looking images. Just think what else they could do. It... it scares me. And I can't help but wonder why."

Victoria bit her lip. The situation scared her, too. Not the emails, but the spiralling situation she found herself in as a result of them. Deep down, she knew Holly was right. They needed to work together to find the perpetrators, but that meant being apart.

"I love you," she whispered.

"I love you too, more than anything." Holly gently placed a hand on her cheek and moved her head into position in order to softly kiss her. Victoria didn't know when she'd have Holly in her arms again, and she wasn't going to be satisfied with some innocent peck.

She took Holly's face in her hands and pressed their lips together in a fusion of adoration and determination. Whoever was attempting to destroy their relationship had just succeeded in making it stronger. Victoria relished the idea of bringing the person down. In fact, for however long this project took, she'd live off it.

CHAPTER ELEVEN

HOLLY DROPPED her bag to the floor and looked around the hotel room. Her suitcase from earlier still sat on the luggage rack. Unpacking felt like making the arrangement unwelcomingly permanent. Living out of her suitcase made the horrible experience seem a lot more temporary.

The hotel was nice, a four-star in Manhattan. It was close to the Upper West Side house she shared with Victoria, but it felt like a million miles away. She trudged farther into the room and stared at the coffeemaker on the desk.

It was midnight, but she knew sleep wouldn't be coming anytime soon. Exhaustion played with her eyelids, but she knew her brain was too busy with questions. Rest wouldn't come to her until she had at least started to work on the problem of who was behind the images.

She grabbed a coffee pod and angrily shoved it into the top of the machine. She placed a cup under the spout and pressed the button. The machine sprang to life, whirring and vibrating as if it were about to take off into the air.

Moving out may have been Holly's idea, but that didn't

mean she liked it. In fact, she hated every second of it. She was away from her home, her family, her lover.

She closed her eyes and pictured Victoria lying in their bed at home. She knew sleep wouldn't come easily for Victoria that night either.

Holly picked up her bag and pulled out her laptop, a fresh notepad, and some pens. She placed them on the desk and stared at her reflection in the mirror.

"Who would do this?" she asked herself. "And why?"

She shook her head. It was too broad a question. Knowing why someone would do something was a tremendous undertaking; it often involved a deep personal knowledge of that person—impossible when she was confronted with a list of everyone they'd ever spoken to as suspects.

No, the real question in a case such as this was who *could* do this?

She sat down, opened her journal and started writing a list. People Victoria worked with, people Holly worked with. Friends and family. Everyone went on the list, in no particular order and with no immediate passes.

Holly knew she needed to approach this as she would any other news article. She couldn't let her personal feelings get in the way. She wrote until she developed a cramp in her right hand. Four pages of names sat in front of her as well as a big question mark which indicated the big unknown, the person they didn't know but who knew them.

That one frightened Holly the most.

She picked up the coffee mug, the machine having stopped its dramatic display a while ago. Sipping on the drink, she picked up a highlighter pen and ran it through the people she knew the least. The people who Victoria mentioned but Holly had yet to meet.

To eliminate those people, Holly would have to rely on Victoria's ability to read their behaviour. A tall order.

"What do we know?" Holly asked her reflection. "They know my email address, they can create elaborate hoaxes, they want to frame Victoria, possibly Ashley... or maybe she was just a convenient fall guy. They know about the power of attorney. And, most of all, they want us apart."

She tapped the pen against her lip.

"They want us apart. Or at least for me to doubt Victoria." She stood up and paced. "But that could have been achieved another way. This much effort is bizarre. It can't just be someone who is romantically interested in either of us."

She stood in front of the ceiling-to-floor window and looked out at the sparkling lights of New York. She tossed the conundrum over and over in her mind, trying to figure out the angle.

Someone wanted her to doubt Victoria. If she hadn't known Victoria so well, she might have fallen for it. An involuntary shiver rushed up her spine. If they'd picked something else, something less radical, she might very well have fought with Victoria for real.

She spun away from the view and shook her head. Thinking like that wouldn't help her at all; she needed to be detached and objective. She needed to think about what steps to take to unravel the mystery.

She needed to look deeper into the faked images and see where they led. She needed an expert.

CHAPTER TWELVE

VICTORIA STEPPED out of the elevator and walked through the *Arrival* offices. She held her head high and kept a determined step.

She'd never been a good actress and had never been good at reading people. Neither had ever been required of her; now she was expected to do both with some confidence.

She had to appear upset, which wouldn't be a stretch because that was exactly how she felt. Someone was pulling strings and playing games, and Victoria wanted to tear the office apart until she found them. If she didn't find them in *Arrival,* then she'd take to the streets of New York. She'd go as far as she needed to put a stop to the madness.

Holly had other ideas. Ideas that involved subterfuge and a more measured approach. Ideas that would probably be much more successful than the trail of destruction Victoria would prefer to leave in her wake, in her search for the perpetrator.

She walked into her outer office and tossed her coat at Claudia.

"Move my appointment with Lars to tomorrow, tell Colin I need to see updated figures within the hour, take Izzy to be groomed—today. And take off that awful scarf. You look like Beethoven."

Claudia opened and closed her mouth a few times in shock before muttering an apology and clutching at the silky monstrosity around her neck.

"Louise," she called as she entered her office.

A few seconds later, Louise appeared with a notepad and pencil in hand.

"Cancel my dinner reservation for Friday," she said, putting her bag by the side of her desk and looking through the mail.

"Of course, Victoria. Would you like me to rebook?"

"Why would I attend a romantic restaurant alone? Unless you can manage to convince Holly to return to my side." She looked up at Louise, doing her best to maintain a passive expression. "No? Then, no, just cancel the reservation."

"O-of course. Anything else?"

"No." She sat down and opened the envelope at the top of the pile. She heard Louise walk away. She got a small, black leather notebook out of her bag and picked up her Montblanc fountain pen from her desk. She made a note of what she had said and what Louise's reply had been.

There were probably undertones that she hadn't detected. She'd told Holly it was going to be an impossible task for her to notice anything untoward in anyone's behaviour as she quite frankly never spent any time looking at their behaviour to notice any changes.

A log of all of her interactions was essential, even though it was going to be a criminal waste of her precious time.

Still, she'd do whatever it took to resolve the mystery and have Holly back at home. She'd just taken the first step, announcing the breakup. Well, in the only way Victoria Hastings possibly would announce such a thing.

The wheels were in motion; now she'd just have to wait.

CHAPTER THIRTEEN

HOLLY WAITED on the perfectly manicured grounds of Hugo and Alexia's school. The perfectly manicured lawn and the children in flawlessly pressed uniforms did not provide the best backdrop for the awkward conversation she was about to have.

They may not have been her biological children, but they meant as much to her as if they had been. To Holly, they were a family unit, and the fact that someone was messing with them, and therefore effecting the lives of her children, angered her to no end.

A familiar Town Car pulled up on the driveway, amongst the other luxury vehicles.

Holly took a deep breath to calm her nerves. Alexia had a sixth sense when something was wrong and when she was being lied to. In some respects, the girl was the exact replica of her mother; in others she was the polar opposite. Holly couldn't help but think she would go very far in whatever she chose to do with her life.

Hugo noticed Holly first, then gestured to Alexia. They approached and Holly felt her heart thumping in her chest.

"What are you doing here?" Alexia asked. "Why were you not at home this morning?"

Holly and Victoria had agreed that they would say that Holly was working that morning to save Victoria from a barrage of difficult questions. Unfortunately, the youngest Hastings didn't seem to have accepted that.

Holly wrapped an arm around Alexia's shoulders, gesturing with her head for Hugo to stand on her other side.

"I came to tell you that I'm staying somewhere else for a few days," she began.

"What did Mom do?" Hugo asked immediately.

"Nothing, it was me," Holly said. "I'm not going to go into it all with you, it's between your mother and me, but I wanted to tell you that I love you both very much and I will be back very soon. This is just a temporary thing; I'm giving your mother some space."

"Why don't you just stay in the guest room?" Alexia asked.

"Because that's not enough space."

"That's silly," Alexia said. "What if I need to talk to you?"

"Then you can call me, text me, video-chat me, email me…" Holly chuckled. "Whatever you like, I'll always be there for you, you know that."

Alexia looked crestfallen. "But I want you at home with us. What about movie night? Will you come to movie night?"

Holly shook her head. "No, I'm sorry, honey. I have to stay away for a little while."

"Did you argue?" Hugo asked.

"I bet Mom said something," Alexia added, looking up at her brother.

"She didn't," Holly reassured. "Your mother isn't to blame. I am."

Hugo looked unconvinced, and Alexia looked broken. Holly had known the conversation would be difficult, but she had no idea it would be this tough.

"I'm just so sorry that you have to be involved in this. And that I have to ask you a favour," she said.

"What?" Alexia asked.

"If anyone asks, you need to say, 'No comment.' You know how the press will be if they find out that we're having a break. They'll hound your mom more than usual. So, try not to say anything to anyone. And… be nice to your mom. This really isn't her fault."

"What did you do?" Hugo asked, suspicion lacing his tone.

"I promise that I'll tell you everything when I move back in. I just… I just can't go into it all now. And please don't try to wheedle it out of your mom either."

They both nodded, albeit reluctantly, and Holly squeezed them close to her. She wanted to tell them the truth, but she couldn't risk the plan. The fewer people who knew the truth about their separation, the less likely there would be a leak in sensitive information. Their breakup needed to look legitimate, without making the children worry that their perfect little world was about to fall apart.

They'd agonised over what to say to Alexia and Hugo,

eventually agreeing on a halfway house between truth and fiction. Not a full breakup, just a break. Even that was almost too much for Holly.

"I love you both, so very much," she whispered, clutching at them.

She'd always known that she loved them, but it was only now that she realised how desperately she *needed* them in her life. Seeing Hugo running around the house searching for his school tie, hearing Alexia complaining about her milk-to-cereal ratio was an important part of her life.

"You promise you'll come home?" Alexia asked.

"I do, I absolutely promise."

The school bell rang, and their time together was cut short. Holly gave them one last squeeze before letting them both go.

"Okay." She wiped at her tears and sniffed. "Okay. You two go and learn stuff. Be good. Remember, I love you. Be good for your mom."

Alexia wrapped her arms around Holly's waist and hung on. Holly softly patted her back, looking up at Hugo who was looking at her curiously. She offered him a tight smile, knowing that he wasn't quite convinced of what she was telling him yet. She couldn't blame him; he was old enough to remember his mother's divorce from his father.

"Come on, we need to go," he said, tugging on Alexia's sleeve.

Alexia sadly pulled away. "I'll text you," she promised Holly.

"Good, just not in class," Holly reminded her. The last thing they needed was another visit to the principal's office.

Alexia nodded, and they both walked towards the building. Holly watched them until they were safely inside and out of sight. Once they were gone, she shoved her hands into her pockets and hurried away.

She had a feeling she was being watched, a feeling that had been with her since the previous afternoon. In some ways she hoped that she was being watched. At least then all of this would be for a reason.

She didn't have to worry about putting on a good show for any potential voyeur. Tears had started to stream down her cheeks.

This can't be over soon enough, she thought.

CHAPTER FOURTEEN

A LIGHT KNOCK on the open door to her office indicated to Victoria that Louise had taken less than fifteen minutes to tell Gideon about her new relationship status. She looked up and raised an eyebrow at the man hovering in the doorway.

"Yes?"

"Are you okay?" he asked, concern evident in his expression.

"Why wouldn't I be?" Victoria lowered her head and returned to marking up copy.

She heard the door close, and a moment later Gideon took a seat in one of the chairs in front of her desk.

"Louise said something," he explained. "Something about Holly?"

Victoria raised her head and jutted out her chin defiantly. "Yes, she's left." She lifted up the article she'd been reviewing. "I have grave doubts about the state of education in this country. This person has allegedly graduated from

Harvard, and yet the correct placement of a comma seems to absolutely elude them."

"Holly's left?" Gideon clarified.

She lowered the article. "Yes, she accused me of being a liar. About what, who can say? She was rather upset and decidedly firm on her decision. By the time I got home last night, she was leaving."

Victoria watched Gideon carefully for his reaction. She wasn't entirely sure what she was looking for, but she'd report everything back to Holly and see if the younger woman could decipher any details that had escaped her.

"You thought she was having an affair," Gideon spoke, his brow furrowed as he tried to piece together what was happening.

"Yes, well, that was ludicrous. Why would Holly ever have an affair?" Victoria attempted to sweep her previous accusations under the carpet. The other day she'd said things she hadn't meant in order to provoke a response from Gideon, to try to hear him confirm how strong their relationship was. It seemed ridiculous now.

She had to backpedal. She didn't want to besmirch Holly's good name, and she had to stick to the story. As far as anyone was supposed to know, Holly left because Victoria was lying about something.

"I really don't have time to discuss this all day, Gideon," she said. "Suffice to say, Holly has left. It was only a matter of time until she did. Whatever ridiculous notion has been put into her head about my character has taken root, and she made it quite clear that she wouldn't be willing to discuss it any further with me. But I have a job to do, a magazine to put out. So, if you're quite ready to get back to work?"

Victoria lowered her head, pretending to focus back on the article. In actual fact she was trying to control her swirling emotions. Things were feeling very real and very raw. Holly had left her, if only temporarily, and as part of some grand scheme. But that didn't make her feel any less injured by the split.

"Of course, if you want to speak to her, then please be my guest," she added. Holly would have far more luck analysing people than Victoria could hope for personally. Holly's journalistic instincts and her ability to accurately pinpoint any falsehoods and root out any unusual behaviour was something Victoria could never hope to replicate.

"Victoria," Gideon said softly, "is there anything I can do for you? I know how much Holly meant to you."

She gritted her teeth at his use of the past tense. She closed her eyes and focused on a couple of breaths to try to calm herself down. She didn't think Gideon was so good an actor as to be able to offer such genuine-sounding support if he was in any way involved in the forgeries. Although, Holly had been quick to warn her not to trust anyone. Not even Gideon.

Victoria would never be accused of wearing her heart on her sleeve, but the knowledge that she had absolutely no one to confide in was already becoming overwhelming. And she was only fifteen minutes into the workday.

If she was going to get through the day, she needed to push everyone away and focus fully on her work.

"I'm fine," she ground out. "Well, aside from the fact

that it seems impossible to find a feature writer who can spell."

"You know where I am if you need me," he said.

She continued to gaze at the papers on her desk, not really seeing them as she mentally tracked Gideon's departure. Once he was gone, she let out a small sigh. It was going to be a tremendously tough day at the office.

CHAPTER FIFTEEN

VICTORIA APPROACHED the reception desk and let out a long and heartfelt sigh.

"We meet again, Terry," she greeted the employee of the self-storage company.

"Hello, Miss Hastings," he replied with a gormless grin on his face.

The entire charade was ridiculous, but Victoria was willing to jump through any hoops if it meant getting Holly back in her life as quickly as possible.

Terry slid a key with a large, wooden block attached to it across the table top and issued some directions. Victoria remembered the way. She'd visited the dingy storage centre three times to pick up Holly's belongings, and the memory of the first time they'd found the storage room was etched into her memory forever.

Holly had been so excited to discover that she'd been in the process of moving when she'd travelled to Paris, and all her belongings had been safely tucked away in a storage room for the year she'd been gone. Clothes, photos, books,

CDs, and all manner of personal effects had been thrown into the storage room, often in black sacks.

The real highlight had been the discovery of Holly's journals, something Victoria hadn't even known existed.

She snatched up the key and walked down the corridors. In the back of her mind, a thought lingered that she was perhaps walking into a trap. An anonymous email which just said, "A16, 6pm," had sent her scuttling from her office.

A16 was the storage locker number, and Victoria had naturally assumed it was a message from Holly. Only now did she wonder if it might have been from someone else.

She approached the metal roller door of A16 and knew that on the other side of the door was either Holly or the person responsible for whatever was happening. As far as she was concerned, it was win-win. Either the love of her life or her mortal enemy would be in there. She smirked at the thought of murdering them with her own bare hands.

The padlock was missing, which confirmed that someone was inside. She took a deep breath, bent down, and grabbed hold of the handle. She closed her eyes for a brief moment and then quickly stood up and opened the roller door.

She blinked and took a step inside.

"Oh, is it six already?" Holly asked with barely a glance from the whiteboard she was scribbling on. "Come in, close the door."

Victoria closed the roller door again and then turned her attention to the room. Inside were two scruffy office chairs, a folding table, some boxes of paperwork, and three whiteboards on stands.

"Let me just finish this," Holly said distractedly, looking at a piece of paper in her hand and then writing on the whiteboard with a marker pen.

Victoria looked around the storage room with fascination. Holly had been busy; she'd converted the empty space into a working office.

Holly finished her task and abruptly turned around, crossed the room, and pulled Victoria into a passionate kiss. Before she had the proper chance to reciprocate, Holly was gone again. Her lover crouched on the floor, opening a sports bag. She produced a towel from inside and unfolded it, placing it on one of the chairs and gesturing for Victoria to sit down.

"There, nice and clean," Holly said.

"I like what you've done with the place," Victoria gestured around the sterile room.

Holly ignored the sarcasm. "It's my war room."

"Why is my mother's name on your whiteboard?" Victoria asked, pointing to the middle of the second one. "In fact, why is most of my family on your whiteboard?"

"Suspects," Holly explained. She plopped down into the second chair, a notepad on her lap. "Until we know better, they are on the list. Remember? No free passes."

"My mother is eighty-two," Victoria reminded her.

"You said yourself that she's not to be trusted," Holly said.

Victoria closed her mouth. She had said that, and it was true. Her mother was rigid in her opinions and fought hard to manipulate people into doing her bidding. She wasn't happy that Victoria had chosen to date a woman nearly half her age, so maybe she deserved to be on the board.

"How did it go at *Arrival*?" Holly asked.

Victoria shrugged a shoulder and looked to the floor. "Difficult," she admitted.

"Do they know?"

"Yes, I let it slip to Louise as soon as I arrived. She seemed surprised, but I couldn't be sure. Gideon appeared within a quarter of an hour to ask if I was all right. He seemed genuine, but…"

Victoria could feel Holly's eyes on her but maintained her appraisal of the concrete floor. She didn't have anything to add. This wasn't her forte, and they both knew it. Asking Victoria to detect any subtle changes in her employees' moods was like asking time to stop sweeping by.

"Okay, that's a good start," Holly said. "I spoke with the kids."

Victoria winced. She wasn't looking forward to returning home and having to field their questions. Especially Alexia's.

"And, I think…" Holly trailed off, allowing silence to fill the room.

"You think?" Victoria looked up, worried at what might come next.

"I might be… being… followed," Holly confessed.

Victoria jumped to her feet. "That's it. No more. You're coming home, and we're getting security. I'm not taking any more chances."

Holly stood up and softly took Victoria by her upper arms. "I could be wrong," she said. "Maybe I'm being paranoid."

"Paranoia is good," Victoria told her. "Worrying keeps us alive."

"I don't think that's necessarily true."

"How are you not more worried about this?" Victoria demanded, shocked by Holly's casual demeanour.

Holly took a step back and gestured to the board. "Someone on this board is to blame, and I'm including the question mark in that statement. I don't think they want to hurt us, just keep an eye on us."

"How can you be sure?"

"Because if they wanted to hurt me, then they would have done it already. Why go through the hassle of making and sending those images? They're messing with us on an emotional level."

Victoria pinched the bridge of her nose and turned around to give herself a couple of seconds' peace. She hated the whole situation from top to bottom, but she had to agree with Holly. This was psychological warfare.

The fact that someone had created and sent the images to Holly was enough to make Victoria's blood boil, but the reality was that she had no idea what else they were capable of. What would they do next? At least now this person thought they were split up; hopefully it would stop until they could track the culprit down.

"Are you any further in finding out who is behind all this?" Victoria slowly turned around and regarded Holly with as calm an expression as she could manage.

"Nothing concrete. But I have discovered that faked images leave markers," Holly explained. "I have a friend looking into that, as well as the location where the emails were sent from. They were anonymous, but nothing online is truly untraceable. We'll find something."

"So, what next?" Victoria was almost afraid to ask.

"I keep investigating," Holly said.

"And you will presumably continue to stay in some seedy motel in the bad part of town?" Victoria asked.

"Yes, I've made friends with all the drug pushers," Holly replied. "They're nice guys, just misunderstood."

Victoria sniffed at being ridiculed and walked over to the whiteboard to examine it in more detail. Holly had written a lot of names; some she didn't even recognise. This wasn't necessarily surprising as Victoria didn't often waste her time remembering people's names.

"I miss you," she whispered, her back to Holly.

"I miss you, too," Holly said.

She felt Holly's arms wrap around her middle, and she sank into the embrace.

"We'll be able to meet here, as long as we're careful about not being followed," Holly explained.

Victoria didn't like the idea of sneaking around, especially to see her own partner, but she knew she didn't have a choice.

"You'll email again?" Victoria asked.

"Yes, I'll send you an anonymous message with a time."

Victoria held back the bitter comment about that strategy not exactly being conducive to her packed schedule, but she knew Holly couldn't help it. Neither of them had chosen this, and if she had to reschedule a meeting with some of the incompetents in the office in order to catch a few minutes with Holly, then she would.

"Shouldn't we just contact the police?" Victoria asked through a sigh.

Holly raised a hand and pointed to the whiteboard.

Victoria followed her outstretched finger and read a few names. Then her eyes settled on it, the chief of police.

"What's that traitorous buffoon doing on the list?" Victoria asked.

"He doesn't like you, because you call him a traitorous buffoon," Holly explained as though this were obvious.

"Well, he is." Victoria wasn't about to give the man a free pass simply because she needed him to be competent at his job for five minutes.

"I know, but it means that going to the police isn't really our first option. Not unless things get more serious or we really can't crack it ourselves. I don't think the police will care that much anyway, do you?"

She shrugged and nodded. She'd hardly endeared herself to the police department over the years. Living in the middle of the city was convenient, but it also meant there were a lot of things to complain about, crime levels being one of them. And Victoria wasn't known for being a quiet soul at the local council meetings. It was one of the few things she made time for outside of work, being of the opinion that the City was falling apart at the seams and being determined to do her part to hold it together.

"Is the hotel treating you well?" Victoria enquired.

"It is." Holly gave her middle one last squeeze before letting her go and walking over to the table to look at the paperwork again.

Victoria sucked in her cheek and looked at Holly's back. It was clear that she wasn't going to tell her the location of the hotel.

This annoyed Victoria in two ways: firstly, the assumption that she couldn't be trusted with sensitive information;

secondly, the fact that Holly was correct to think that she couldn't be trusted.

Victoria had already bookmarked a food hamper that she had found online. It would be the perfect gift for Holly while she stayed in whatever rancid accommodation she had decided upon.

"We need to come up with a scheme so I can speak to Louise. I need to see if she's acting suspiciously," Holly said.

"Agreed. The sooner we can eliminate her from our enquiries, the better. I'd like to have my first assistant back without constantly looking at her and wondering if I should be murdering her."

"I have an idea on that subject," Holly said. She turned around and levelled a look at Victoria. "But, before that, I have one other item of business."

Holly closed the gap between them in two strides before pulling Victoria into another searing kiss. Victoria almost heard the gears in her brain crunching at the sudden change in direction. She recovered quickly and held Holly tightly around the waist, putting every ounce of feeling she could into returning the kiss.

After a few moments, Holly pulled her lips away and started to worship Victoria's neck. Her pulse sped up; having Holly lavish hot, wet kisses on her throat always sent her wild.

"This is temporary, I'll be back before you know it," Holly whispered in between kisses. "And you better be prepared, because I miss you."

Stress fell from Victoria's shoulders like a set of weights falling to the ground. She'd needed to hear that, more than she knew.

"I'm glad to hear it," she returned, her breathing ragged. "But you have to stop what you're doing because I refuse to engage in carnal activities in a damp and dusty storage locker."

Holly slumped against her, her shoulders shaking.

"Are you laughing at me?" Victoria demanded.

"I am," Holly confirmed. She stood up and wiped at the happy tears in her eyes. "Never change, Victoria. Never change."

"Why would I?" she asked in confusion. "What a thing to say. Now, who was next on the list?"

CHAPTER SIXTEEN

HOLLY JOLTED awake to the sound of her mobile phone ringing. She blinked a couple of times before remembering why she was in a hotel room, alone. She'd been in the middle of a wonderful dream where she was on a luxury beach holiday with Victoria, Hugo, and Alexia. Now she was staring at the plain white ceiling of her hotel room. The contrast rejuvenated her desire to solve the mystery and get her life back.

She snatched up the phone and saw an *Arrival* number she recognised all too well. It was Louise.

Holly sucked in a deep breath before answering. "Hello?"

"Ah, you're there. You took your time," Louise said, her attitude cranked up to eleven. "Victoria has asked me to get your key to the house back."

Holly swallowed. They'd agreed on this the previous evening in the war room. It was the ideal way for Holly to get a chance to speak with Louise and decide for herself if there was anything different about her behaviour.

But now that the call was happening, Holly felt a cold shiver run down her spine. It felt all too real.

"I'll drop it off at the house," she said.

"No," Louise said, a perverse pleasure clear in her tone. "No, I want you to deliver it to me personally, so I know it's done. You can come to the office, but don't come up. Of course. I'll meet you in reception. Oh, and I'll take your security pass from you as well."

"Don't sound like you're enjoying this too much, Louise. You'll burst," Holly commented.

"It's nice to know that everything is getting back to normal again," Louise replied. "That this… bizarre world is finally done with. I knew you'd mess it up eventually."

Holly bit her lip to keep from saying what she really wanted to the snotty woman. Louise had played nice while Holly had been with Victoria, but Holly always knew it was an act. Louise had hated her when she had slowly become Victoria's favourite of the two of them. It was all coming out now, but Holly knew she had to manage the conversation if she was going to get anything out of it other than Louise's gloating.

"Actually, I didn't mess anything up," Holly said. "Victoria is the one who did all of this."

Louise stalled for a moment before saying, "I'm really not interested in the details of your lovers' quarrel. Come to the office this afternoon with the key and your pass. I assume you don't have anything better to do? I think it's best that we just put all of this behind us as soon as possible. Yes?"

Holly quickly agreed to Louise's plan, and they ended

the call. She sat up in bed and gently tapped the corner of her phone against her mouth, deep in thought.

Louise had assumed that Holly had messed up, and she'd seemed a little taken aback at the news that it was Victoria who had done so instead. If she was involved, then she'd know that the photos indicated Victoria having an affair, so why put the blame for the relationship ending at Holly's door?

It was a big indication that Louise was not involved. Victoria would be pleased.

Holly wasn't. She'd thought Louise's hero worship of Victoria and hatred of Holly made her the number one suspect.

"Crap," she muttered.

Holly realised that she had been holding on dearly to the suspicion that Louise was involved. It would have been the cleanest and simplest solution. Louise would want to push Holly away but not cause Victoria any real damage in the terms of her image or business standing. If it had been Louise, then they were safe in the knowledge that the images were unlikely to be leaked.

Holly pressed her lips together. She'd make a proper decision on Louise's involvement when she saw her that afternoon, but it was looking very unlikely that she was the culprit.

She looked at her phone again and swiped along her contacts until she came to the only person who might be able to help. She pressed her thumb down on the name and put the phone to her ear. It rang a few times before being answered.

"Too early, Carter."

"I'm sorry, Jazz," Holly apologised. "I just needed to know if you'd had time to look at those emails I sent you?"

Holly had called the computer genius as soon as she started properly investigating the case. Jazz was good at their job and could be trusted. Jazz was also very busy, and Holly had been told that Jazz would get to it when they could.

"No, but I can tell that I'm going to get no sleep until I do. I have a few jobs this morning. Why don't you come over this afternoon?"

Holly jumped to her feet with excitement. A space in Jazz's diary wasn't an easy thing to come by.

"I'll be there, name the time."

"Four. Bring food."

"I will bring all the food," Holly promised. "Thanks, Jazz. I really appreciate this."

"Yeah, yeah," Jazz said sleepily. "I'm going back to bed, see you at four. Oh, by the way, Thai food is good."

Jazz disconnected the call, and Holly let out a sigh of relief. She'd worked with Jazz a few times in the past; they were fantastic at their work but difficult on a personal level. Jazz had their pick of computer work. If your project didn't interest them, then they didn't take it on. This would have been a problem for Holly because she didn't know many hackers—certainly not ones she could trust.

She tossed her phone on the bed and stretched up high to try to release the tension from her back. The bed was nice, but it wasn't up to Victoria's standards. Every day that passed made her appreciate more and more the homely luxury that she lived in. It wasn't just that Victoria was rich; they didn't have a golden toilet or anything ridiculous like that. It was just that the townhouse felt like a home, with its muted colours and elegant, soft furnishings. The hotel, no matter how spectacular, just couldn't compete with home.

Thinking like that wasn't helping. If she wanted to get back home, she needed to crack on.

"Okay, let's get today started," she said to herself, realising that she was now a person who spoke to herself.

CHAPTER SEVENTEEN

VICTORIA TAPPED the tip of her Montblanc fountain pen against her lip. She'd finally signed off on the final draft of *Arrival*, and it had been sent to the printers. It was usually a time for quiet rejoicing, but now it just cracked open enough of her schedule to allow her to dwell on what was happening outside of work.

She'd never been exactly close to any of her employees, but she was now finding that she trusted none of them. Holly's conspiracy theory mindset had completely pervaded her usually balanced view. Now, every single word or action was overthought to maddening levels.

It was only the second day of the subterfuge, and already Victoria found herself driven insane by the situation.

Her thoughts were firmly set on Louise. Upon arriving at the office, Victoria had ordered Louise to get the key to the townhouse from Holly. Louise had quickly assured her that she'd take care of everything. She'd followed Victoria into her office and told her that she would manage the situation; she also informed her that she had found a gap in her schedule for a quick shoulder massage.

It was a gesture Victoria was unused to seeing in Louise, and the kindness she found in her eyes made Victoria pause. Was Holly right? Was her first assistant a prime suspect? And if she was, what was her goal?

She tossed the heavy pen down onto her notepad and clutched her head in frustration. She took a couple of deep breaths; she'd not find out anything concrete by running her brain in circles.

She lowered her hands and wiggled her shoulders a little to relieve some of the pressure. She had a job to do. Not producing the next issue of *Arrival*, no, that could wait a little while longer. Instead, a major suspect on Holly's master list was photographer Phoebe Wheeler.

Phoebe had the skillset required to manipulate images. She also had a wealth of stock images of both Victoria and Ashley from which to create such images. A motive wasn't clear, but Holly had already explained that motive wasn't always entirely clear from the outset.

Oh, how Victoria missed Holly and their discussions. Victoria loved her children, but being a single parent meant that she was rarely challenged during conversations. Her opinion had been the only one that mattered until Holly had arrived on the scene, with her own way of seeing the world and her endless supply of patience in explaining things to Victoria.

She'd never admit it, but Holly made her a better person. She'd opened her eyes to other people, cultures,

ways of life, politics, and more. She wasn't changing funda-
mentally as a person, but she was able to see the broader
picture.

The house was quiet without Holly. Especially with the
children walking on eggshells around her.

Victoria reached over to her phone and pressed the
intercom button.

"Ask Phoebe Wheeler to come and see me," she
instructed.

As chance would have it, Victoria had a perfectly valid
reason to speak with Phoebe. Now she needed to try to
fathom a way to question her without seeming like she was
doing so.

Holly had eluded to some details in her journals that
had her suspecting Phoebe of possible involvement. She
wouldn't clarify why, which led Victoria to fear the worst.
Had they been an item? Had Phoebe made a move on
Holly?

Just like that, Phoebe had gone from a talented and
loyal photographer to a potential snake in the grass
overnight. Victoria fought to not grind her teeth in frustration at the images her mind conjured.

"She's on her way up now," Claudia replied.

Victoria refreshed her email, hoping for information on
her next meeting with Holly. She'd been steadily refreshing
the application every few minutes for the last four hours.

So far, there was nothing.

It was frustrating, to say the least, that she wasn't able to
contact Holly, or even know where she was at that moment
in time. Life without Holly was a strange feeling, and

Victoria found it disagreed with her immensely. It dawned on her that her relationship wasn't as stable as she'd thought. That was something she was determined to fix.

"You wanted to see me?" Phoebe asked, standing in the doorway.

Unlike most of the other *Arrival* minions, Phoebe was confident and collected. She didn't shy away under Victoria's stern gaze. She was good at her job, and she knew it.

"Yes, come in, close the door." Victoria gestured to the seat in front of her desk. She passed over an open copy of a competitor magazine and waited for Phoebe to pick it up.

When she did, she laughed. "This is blatant copying."

"It is," Victoria agreed. "Still, it's supposed to be flattering, isn't it?"

"Having your ideas stolen?" Phoebe asked, her eyes still roaming over the two-page spread. "I suppose. I'd just like to be the one stealing ideas for once, rather than having to come up with all the ideas."

Victoria chuckled. "It occurs to me, if they want to copy us, let's make them pay for it. I want you to come up with something big for the Dolce spread. Something that will cost them money to replicate, a huge splash."

She looked out of the office door and tracked Louise's movements. Her first assistant was wearing a knockoff Chanel suit that some might consider similar to the original she had worn two weeks ago.

"They say that imitation is the sincerest form of flattery," Victoria said. "So, let's make imitation an expensive business."

She could see the cogs turning in Phoebe's mind. Victoria was aware that it was dangerous to give a creative personality free range with the company credit card, but she knew she'd make it back and more if Phoebe pulled it off. The competitors wouldn't be able to stomach the loss.

It was cutthroat, and she liked it.

"I'll come up with something," Phoebe promised.

"Wonderful. Also, I was wondering if you'd have time to speak with the toddlers who run the social media department? We get a lot of traction on Instagram, but some of the compositions they come up with make my skin crawl. They need an artistic lesson, if you have time?"

"I'd love to. I've seen a few posts that could use some work. I'll get in touch with Meghan."

Victoria nodded. "I'd like to be a part of that meeting; I need to know more about that platform. Holly had said she'd show me, but…"

She trailed off, pursed her lips, and looked at the paperwork on her desk.

"But?" Phoebe ventured, confusion clear in her tone.

Victoria looked at her. "Oh, you've not heard? I would have assumed tales of my status would have travelled like a Millennial towards a smashed avocado on rye. Holly and I are no more."

Phoebe's expression was unreadable. "Oh, I'm sorry to hear that."

She lightly shrugged a shoulder. "She was young and naïve, I should never have gotten into a relationship with someone so… flighty."

"I agree," Phoebe said.

Victoria clenched her fist in her lap, willing the anger to die down quickly.

"You're better off without her, honestly. Some of these

youngsters are so entitled and impossible. Holly was a nice girl, but you can do so much better."

Victoria hoped that she was managing to keep the surprise from her face. Phoebe hadn't hesitated; she'd immediately been happy about their separation. Victoria hadn't said why they had broken up or what her feelings were towards the matter. She'd had a whole speech prepared, but it was unnecessary as Phoebe had rushed in with her thoughts.

Victoria was admittedly terrible at reading people, but even she could tell that this was unusual behaviour. Surely?

"Quite," she managed to say. "Anyway, I won't keep you."

Phoebe stood up. "I'll liaise with Claudia and Meghan to find a suitable time for this meeting. And I'll get back to you about Dolce first thing Monday morning."

Victoria simply nodded, finding words difficult to come by. Phoebe didn't seem to notice her confusion as she left the office.

Victoria watched her leave. She snatched up her notepad and started jotting down some notes on the surreal conversation. Why would anyone think that she and Holly were not the perfect match? In fact, why were people not surprised that they had broken up? It was as if they had simply been awaiting the time when everything fell apart.

It angered Victoria that her relationship with Holly was viewed as temporary or ill-advised. As soon as they were back together, Victoria would ensure that people knew how committed they were to one another. There would never be a question in their minds as to how well they fit together as a couple.

How she'd do that, she had no idea.

CHAPTER EIGHTEEN

HOLLY TURNED from the sidewalk into the shadowy alleyway. She eyed the trashcans and peered into the shadows of the fire escape stairwells to be sure no one was lurking there. It was the middle of the day, but you could never tell.

Especially now that she was thoroughly paranoid about everything.

She climbed a set of metal stairs and knocked on the door. The black paint was peeling, and the lock was so badly scratched and worn that the door looked abandoned. No one would suspect that anyone lived beyond it, which was probably exactly what Jazz was hoping for.

Holly heard the sound of movement, and then the sliding of the cover on the peephole. She smiled and held up the takeout bag.

The door opened, and Jazz gestured for her to hurry up and come inside.

"Thanks for seeing me," Holly said once she was in the cramped, dimly lit hallway.

"That's Thai food, right?" Jazz asked, taking the brown bag from Holly's arms.

Holly barely had time to reply before Jazz left. She blew out a breath, removed her coat, and hung it up on one of the nails sticking out of the wall which acted as a makeshift coatrack. If something that had clearly been around for years could be considered makeshift.

Holly followed Jazz into the main room of the apartment. It had grown since the last time she had been there: an extra desk with machinery and equipment sat beside the enormous table that housed four large computer monitors. Above them sat an array of shelves with computers and external fans whirring away.

A sofa with a large television completed the furnishings.

Jazz was in the modest kitchen, plating up food.

"You want?" Jazz asked, indicating a box with a chopstick.

"No, I've eaten," Holly said. She'd learnt her lesson from a previous visit. Jazz could put away large amounts of food and didn't particularly like to share.

There were two chairs set up in front of the computer screens, a beaten-up and yet luxurious office chair with padded armrests, and a foldable wooden chair with a slat missing.

Holly sat on the wooden chair and looked at the screen. The doctored image of Victoria and Ashley was on display, large and in high quality. Despite knowing it was a fake, Holly found it no easier to look at.

"It's a fake," Jazz said, walking into the room while precariously balancing an enormous plate of food in their hand.

"I know," Holly said.

"She your girlfriend?" Jazz asked.

"Yes."

Jazz sat down and nodded. "Nice. Victoria Hastings, editor-in-chief of some big deal fashion magazine, right?"

"*Arrival*, yes."

"Never read it."

"You're not really the target market," Holly pointed out.

Jazz laughed. "No, I'm really not. I've done some research, though. It's big on LGBT rights. Not surprising if the chief is…" Jazz looked at Holly and smirked.

Holly pointed at the image. "Does it have to be so big?"

Jazz sat forward and pressed a couple of buttons on one of the three keyboards on the desk. The image vanished.

"Sorry, didn't think. It's a fake, but it's a very good one. I couldn't see any of the usual markers. Whoever did it is a very clean worker," Jazz explained.

Holly bit back a sarcastic retort which would have been more at home coming from Victoria's lips. "Any idea who did it?"

"Nope. There's not a lot to go on in the image, so I started to focus on the emails. They are sophisticated, I got bounced around a lot, but I managed to find the source."

"You did?" Holly sat up straight.

"You're not going to like it," Jazz warned.

"Tell me," Holly demanded.

"*Arrival*."

"What?" Holly's eyes widened.

"The emails were sent from somewhere in the *Arrival* offices. I can't tell where exactly, but whoever sent these either works for or has access to a computer plugged into the *Arrival* mainframe."

Holly felt her jaw drop open. She'd been right. It was someone at *Arrival*. But that didn't make it any less shocking or horrible. She suddenly thought of Victoria, working side by side with the perpetrator. A shiver ran down her spine.

"Can you find out anything else from the emails?" she asked.

Jazz tilted their head from side to side in thought. "Maybe, dunno yet. I need to look into it and see what else I can shake loose."

Holly worried her lip. She'd cut her suspect list in half, but she didn't feel any better about things. In fact, she felt worse. The knowledge that she was getting closer just made her feel more fearful.

"But it definitely came from inside *Arrival?*" Holly clarified.

"One hundred percent," Jazz confirmed.

"Then I need to cross-reference who was in the building at the times I received emails," Holly muttered to herself, coming up with a plan of action.

"I can do that from here," Jazz said, sliding their plate to one side and pulling a keyboard close.

Holly felt her eyebrow raise at the knowledge that Jazz was able to very quickly access *Arrival's* security logs. She knew, of course, that it wasn't legal, but she couldn't find it in her to complain. Jazz was no doubt about to compile a list in a matter of minutes and keystrokes, something that would surely take Holly many hours. And that was if she was able to obtain the data at all.

Jazz's fingers flew over the keyboard. "I'll cross-ref this with the timestamps on the emails and on the server."

"Thanks, that's great."

"Do you know why someone would do this?" Jazz asked.

"No. We can't think of who or why. That's what's really hurtful, the not knowing."

"People do stupid shit," Jazz muttered.

"That's true. But this is really time-consuming stupid shit. Someone must really hate one or both of us to do this," Holly pointed out.

"Or they are trying to protect one of you from the other?" Jazz suggested.

Holly laughed. "Well, it's just bringing us closer together. And why would someone do that anyway?"

"Well, you did have an accident and you lost your memory, and then eighteen months later, you're in a relationship with your former boss who is known for being a dragon." Jazz stopped typing and glanced at Holly.

Holly allowed that to digest for a moment. "Yes, okay, it's a weird setup. I agree. But it works, Victoria is lovely. She's not what you think."

Holly spent a lot of her time telling people that Victoria wasn't at all what they thought she was. It was pretty exhausting. She could understand why people worried about her, but she wished they wouldn't. She was an adult and could make her own decisions, no matter what society thought of her relationship with her former employer.

Jazz held up their hands. "You don't need to justify it to me. I'm just saying it could look weird to some people."

"Then those people need to come and speak to me rather than doing all this," Holly said, anger lacing her tone.

"I agree. I'm just saying there's another avenue of investigation you might want to consider," they said softly.

Holly took a deep breath to try to push her irritation to one side. "You're right, I'm sorry. It's just this is causing a lot of stress. I… I moved out. Just to make it look realistic to whoever is doing this. I mean, if they release these pictures to the press, then Victoria's going to suffer at work. Our kids will as well."

Jazz looked sympathetic and slowly nodded. "I'll do what I can to find whoever it is, Carter."

Holly tried to smile, but she was finding it increasingly difficult as she unpicked more of the mystery. "Thank you."

"Just keep bringing the food." Jazz winked.

Holly chuckled, and Jazz went back to work. Holly watched as the computer genius accessed various things that they probably shouldn't have access to. Holly wasn't going to worry about the legality of anything at the moment; she was too determined to find answers.

Now she needed to arrange another meeting with Victoria, tell her that the suspect resided within *Arrival*, and try to convince her better half to not murder everyone within the building.

CHAPTER NINETEEN

VICTORIA WAS on the phone when she noticed Louise leave the outer office. It wasn't something she'd ordinarily notice, or care about, but all of her senses were homed in on detecting the unusual. As she didn't know what the usual was, it meant she was now hyper-focused on everything.

She continued her call but narrowed her eyes as she watched Louise's retreating form. There was something suspicious about her behaviour.

Her view of Louise was suddenly blocked by Steven entering the outer office. He paused and spoke with Claudia for a moment. Victoria glanced at her schedule. As she thought, she didn't have a meeting with him.

Then again, Steven wasn't exactly known for booking meetings.

She finished up her call the moment he invited himself into her office.

"I have a schedule, you know," she informed him, a smirk on her face.

He looked around the room comically. "Oh, yes, please

excuse me, *everyone*. Is it okay if I take just a few moments of Victoria's time?"

"Such a comedian," she murmured.

He grinned widely and handed her a couple of documents. "I just need you to sign these. I would have put them in the internal mail, but things go missing and I thought I'd stretch my legs. And, of course, it's Friday, so who knows when you would have received them."

She took the papers and glanced at them before picking up her fountain pen.

"I was also going to ask if you wanted to go out for drinks tomorrow evening. You probably don't, but I find myself at a loose end." He flopped into the chair in front of her desk and let out a pathetic sigh. "I'm having to call my department in to work over this weekend, so I'm in everyone's bad books. I'll need something to look forward to in the evening. If you have some time?"

"Actually, I do have some time," Victoria said.

Hugo had asked if he could take Alexia to the cinema that afternoon and then on to somewhere for dinner. Alexia had gone decidedly cold on the idea of spending the day with her, instead asking to go and see a friend.

With the prospect of an empty house looming, Victoria had decided to work on Saturday. Goodness knows she needed the break from the strained silence.

"I have some paperwork to catch up on, so I'll find myself in the office tomorrow as well," she lied.

Holly had yet to be in touch regarding times and dates for any meetings, not that they were planning to meet every night.

"Wonderful, dinner?" He suggested.

She signed the final document and handed the papers back. "Dinner."

"I won't get you in trouble with the missus, will I?" He took the papers and stood up.

"No, I'll tell you about *that* over dinner," she said, noting that the gossip about her love life seemed to only travel a certain number of floors.

He frowned but wisely seemed to sense that it wasn't the right time to wheedle further information from her. He nodded and pointed at her desk phone. "Give me a call when you're ready to head out."

He walked out of the office at the same moment that Claudia walked in.

"Sorry to disturb you, Victoria," she apologised as she handed over a letter that had been couriered. "It's from Chantel."

Chantel was an up-and-coming designer who hated email and had taken to sending handwritten messages over the city via bikes. Apparently, she was saving the environment. Victoria doubted she had considered the lungs of the poor cyclists she employed as they made their way through the grimy city.

She tore at the envelope when she noticed that Claudia was still standing there.

"Yes?" she asked coldly.

Claudia looked deeply uncomfortable but stood her ground. "I… I just wanted to say that I'm sorry about you and Holly. I thought you were a great couple. I hope you work things out."

Victoria didn't get a chance to form a reply before Claudia—wisely—ran from the office. Any other time such impertinence would have been met with blowback of Victoria Hastings proportions. But this was a unique situation, and Victoria found that she was overjoyed to hear from someone who seemed to think they'd been a good match and wished them the best.

So far, aside from Gideon, people had been telling her that it was just a matter of time before things fell apart, that Holly wasn't good enough, that they didn't have anything in common.

All of that might have been helpful if they'd actually broken up. But they hadn't.

Victoria was just as deeply in love with Holly as ever, and, as far as she was concerned, they were the most permanent couple in New York. Their union would be ended by her death and her death alone.

But it seemed that *Arrival* didn't feel that way. Most people who dared to speak to her seemed to think it was a fling, a passing fancy. They didn't understand the depth of her feelings for Holly.

Not that she could blame them. She'd done precisely nothing to convince anyone of her true feelings for her younger girlfriend. She wasn't one for displays of any emotion at all, never mind grand displays of love.

It had only recently occurred to her that she wasn't entirely sure she'd even told Holly how much she meant to her. Holly was spot on when she called Victoria aloof. It was her default setting. She didn't have the desire, or the emotional means, to explain herself. Certainly not to explain her feelings on anything, no matter how deeply they ran.

In all honesty, she'd kept herself a little back from Holly

in order to give the girl some space. Space to run for the hills. Victoria didn't have a clue what Holly saw in her, but she must have seen something because she seemed determined to stay.

Which led Victoria to wonder if she should be giving Holly space. Maybe it was time to admit that she couldn't let Holly go. To confess that she needed Holly in her life. The ridiculous separation reinforced that feeling with every hour that went by.

She picked up her phone and dialled Gideon's number.

She drummed her fingers on the desk, waiting for him to answer. When he did, she spoke immediately. "I've changed my mind; I don't want the spread on heel sizes through the ages. I think we need something more classic. Wedding dresses through the ages."

She slammed the phone down, happy with the new direction for the spread.

CHAPTER TWENTY

HOLLY STOOD BACK and stared at the whiteboard. She'd spent the last couple of hours moving a lot of the data around and adding in everything that Jazz had managed to find. The suspect list looked a lot different now, but there was still a long list of names.

Suddenly the roller door to the storage unit opened. Holly spun around and took a few steps back, shocked that someone was unexpectedly entering the space. Thankfully, she recognised the intruder and let out a breath.

"Victoria!" she admonished.

Victoria stepped into the room and closed the door behind her.

"I told you I'd email you when I had something worth showing you," Holly continued.

She couldn't help but smile even if she was frustrated at her girlfriend's complete inability to follow rules. Victoria quickly moved in front of her, took Holly's face in her hands, and placed a soft kiss to her lips.

"You're always worth seeing," Victoria whispered.

Holly felt her cheeks blush.

"Sweet talker." She softly hit Victoria's shoulder. "You still shouldn't be here, and you gave me a heart attack."

Victoria didn't look apologetic as she scanned the whiteboard. "Cracked the case yet? I see my mother is no longer a suspect."

Holly looked at the whiteboard and bit her lip. She hadn't expected to see Victoria that evening, and so she hadn't prepared a suitable way to explain to her that she was working side by side with the scammer.

It certainly wasn't something she relished explaining.

"Come and sit down," she suggested. She took the clean sheet and draped it over Victoria's chair.

"My sister isn't on the list either. What did they do to earn a pass?" Victoria asked as Holly took her arm and eased her closer to the chair. "You didn't call them, did you? I don't have the energy to speak with either of them this weekend. Besides, I've decided I'm going in to the office tomorrow."

"I had some new information; it put them in the clear." Holly pushed Victoria softly into the seat and then pulled her chair to sit in front of her. She gestured to Victoria's feet and then tapped her lap.

Victoria slid off a heel and placed her foot in Holly's lap, her eagle eye still on the whiteboard behind her. Holly started to massage the proffered foot.

"The emails," she started. "They came from *Arrival*."

Victoria slowly turned to look at her. "From *Arrival*?"

"Yes, I had someone check into it, and the emails came from somewhere in the *Arrival* office. I've cross-referenced them with a list of people who were in the office at the times when all the emails were sent, and don't ask how I got that," she requested.

Victoria's eyebrows rose, but she didn't say anything.

"That's the final list." Holly jutted her head back towards the board. "Somewhere on there is the person who's doing this."

"Why on earth would a person from *Arrival* want to do this?" Victoria asked.

Holly dug her thumbs into Victoria's soft arches and tried to massage away the knots that were permanently in residence from a career in heels.

"I don't know, but we have a place to start." Holly continued the massage, now happy that Victoria had defied her orders and turned up out of the blue.

She was missing her but hadn't felt as though she had enough news to warrant taking her time. She had spent the whole evening hoping that, with just a little more time, she'd have found the culprit and could then tell Victoria. Explaining that the forger was an *Arrival* member of staff was a bitter pill, but one surely better swallowed with the actual identity attached to the news.

But hours had passed, and Holly was no closer to identifying the person at fault, even with Jazz working on the case.

It was nice that Victoria was there. Holly felt that if she closed her eyes it would almost feel as if they were at home on any normal evening.

"This room smells," Victoria said, breaking the mood.

Holly chuckled. "It does. You get used to it."

"I don't think I would," she disagreed.

"Victoria?" Holly said softly, questioningly.

"Yes?"

"I still wonder if this has something to do with my accident."

Victoria looked at her thoughtfully. "What makes you think that?"

Holly was relieved that Victoria hadn't just shot down the idea. She knew it was unlikely, but it was something she just couldn't get out of her head.

"The fact they know about the power of attorney. Who at *Arrival* knows about that? It's not exactly common knowledge. I wonder if they are connected in some way."

Victoria opened and closed her mouth before she took another glance at the whiteboard. "I suppose it could," she admitted. "Or, maybe not. You were a member of staff. You are connected to *Arrival* yourself."

"Paris was an *Arrival* event," Holly pointed out.

She gestured for Victoria to pass up her other foot, which she did. "It's just highlighted for me that my journals stop before I left for Paris, and I don't have anything from that time. I don't know who was there, who travelled with us, what happened. Was there any gossip? I haven't really investigated that time at all."

"It might not be connected," Victoria suggested.

"No, but it's still woken me up to the fact that I have these gaps in my memory. I know you're busy, but could you try to find some schedules, travel details? Just so I can put together the pieces in my mind." Holly dug her fingers into Victoria's feet and massaged.

She furrowed her brow as she thought about the one true point in her memory that was a complete mystery to her. Even though she couldn't remember a time before Paris, she had her journals to tell her everything that happened, and after the accident, she had her memories.

That period in the middle was a painful nothingness.

"Of course," Victoria said softly. "I'll get together everything I can."

Holly nodded but refused to look up. She knew there were tears in her eyes and didn't want Victoria to see them. Her girlfriend was already stressed enough; she didn't need Holly losing her mind on top of everything else.

"Your room was four doors down from mine, on the top floor of the Shangri-La," Victoria explained in a soft tone. Holly realised she'd noticed her tears and was trying her best to recall details from a difficult time over two years ago.

"It was a packed schedule, Paris always is," Victoria continued. "We arrived early the first day, after an overnight flight. I got straight to work with meetings. You accompanied me, of course. Who and where, I can't recall. They all blur together in the end. That first night, we all attended a gathering for Dior. Somewhere in Vendome, perhaps?"

Victoria sighed. Holly looked up and saw her face contorting in annoyance.

"I'm sorry, I'm struggling to remember anything of consequence. It was a very trying visit. The table layout for the gala was wrong. Someone sent me a bunch of roses, roses of all things. Gideon was talking about taking a role at *Vogue*, foolish man. Louise was in a terrible mood because I'd taken you to Paris instead of her. My dress…" She threw her head back and laughed bitterly. "It was a terrible week, and at the end of it… you vanished."

Holly squeezed her feet. "I'm here now."

"Yes, you are." Victoria smiled sadly at her. "Sort of."

"You don't enjoy our clandestine meetings in a storage unit?" Holly joked.

"I do, but sadly I don't have a lot of time. I have to get back to the children so Alexia can continue to subtly question me."

"She's been texting me," Holly admitted. She decided to leave out the fact that Alexia's texts had mainly been about trying to fathom what Victoria might have done wrong and what she could do to fix it. No matter how Holly tried to convince her that her birth mother wasn't to blame, Alexia wasn't buying it.

"I had a meeting with Phoebe Wheeler today," Victoria said. "I told her that we were no longer together, and she seemed very pleased about it. Practically wanted to plan a parade."

Holly quickly tried to recall who Phoebe was. There were so many people who went into making *Arrival*. Some of them she'd met; some of them she hadn't. "Oh, the photographer?"

"Yes."

"I'll do some research on her."

"She was very suspicious."

"Because she was happy that we were apart? Or for other reasons?"

Victoria paused and seemed to consider the matter. "I don't know. She just seemed odd. I wrote everything down as you asked. I'll leave you with the notes."

Holly nodded. She was glad that she had suggested Victoria write everything down. Victoria had a tremendous eye for detail, but for some reason the audible word seemed to evaporate in no time. She didn't listen, or if she did, she didn't retain. When repeating a conversation at a later date, most of the details changed. A written account was the only way to guarantee success.

"I should go. The children will be home soon."

Holly gave Victoria's feet a final squeeze and then let them go. Victoria lowered her legs, slipped her heels back on, and stood up.

"What happened to the dress?" Holly asked.

"Hmm?" Victoria frowned. She picked up her bag and opened it as she looked for something.

"You said something about your dress in Paris?" Holly asked.

"Oh, yes, there was a problem with the hem. Two minutes before I had to leave the hotel room and go down to the car, I noticed the hem had dropped at the front. You were scrambling around on the floor in front of me, trying to pin it up. You were useless, of course."

"Thanks, darling," Holly quipped.

"It was a beautiful gown, red, floor-length. Valentino, naturally." Victoria pulled her car keys out of her handbag, and at the same time a piece of paper fluttered to the ground.

Holly got off her chair, crouched down in front of her, and picked it up. She held it up for Victoria to take. As she did, her vision started to blur. The thought of the red dress, looking up at Victoria, and trying to help saturated her vision. It grew and grew into an intense burst of light, red light.

Through the mess of colour, she could see Victoria looking down at her. And then she could see Victoria in a red gown, shouting instructions into her phone. The images swapped places over and over again, causing Holly to feel dizzy.

"Holly?" she heard Victoria ask, but her voice sounded so distant. "Holly?!"

CHAPTER TWENTY-ONE

"HOLLY?" Victoria could hear the panic in her own voice. As soon as Holly had pitched forward from her kneeling position, Victoria had dropped to her own knees and taken her by the upper arms to hold her upright.

"Holly? Please, talk to me," she begged.

Holly had gone deathly white. Her eyes were wide, and she looked like she was staring straight through Victoria. She gave her a small shake, hoping to bring her back to reality.

Thankfully, it worked.

Holly blinked and started to sit back. "I'm okay," she whispered.

Victoria turned and grabbed her handbag which had been dropped to the floor the instant she realised something was wrong with Holly. She pulled it open and grabbed the small, metal bottle of water she carried with her everywhere. She yanked open the top and held it towards Holly.

"Drink some water," she commanded.

Holly took the bottle and did what she was told.

Victoria trailed her eyes over her, checking for any sign of pain or injury. She had no idea what had just happened, only that it had scared the living daylights out of her.

"I remembered," Holly said, still breathless.

Victoria felt her eyebrows raise. "Remembered what?"

"You… the red dress." Holly let out a shaky breath and turned to face her properly. "It was like a flash of recollection. That's never happened before. It must have been because we were talking about it, and then I was kneeling in front of you, looking up at you, the same as in my memory."

Victoria took the bottle and sipped some water herself. They'd always suspected Holly's memories were intact, but this was the first solid proof they had had.

"We need to get you to the doctor," she said.

"No." Holly shook her head.

Victoria stared at her with incredulity. Holly looked back at her with determination. The colour was returning to her cheeks, and she was looking stronger with every second that passed.

"What can they do? They'll check my vitals and then they'll shrug and say the brain is a mysterious thing."

Victoria opened her mouth to argue but quickly closed it again. Holly was right. They'd long ago agreed that the best medical people in the country knew very little about brain damage and memory loss. At this point, Holly very likely knew more about her own memory loss and recovery than any so-called expert Victoria could find.

"Did you remember anything else?"

Holly shook her head. "No, it was just a flash, a few

seconds. In the hotel room, you in the red dress. Me with a safety pin."

"Are you sure it was a memory? Not just a suggestion brought on by our conversation?" Victoria hated to doubt her, but they had to be sure.

Holly frowned and cocked her head to the side, deep in thought. "The carpet was a dark grey. It made it impossible to find the pins if I put them down. You hadn't put your heels on yet. You had dark red nail polish on. You were on the phone, shouting at someone called Beth? Does that sound right? Or did I make all of that up?"

Victoria furrowed her brow as she tried to recall just what toenail colour she had worn more than two years ago. It sounded right. A faint recollection that she'd been on the phone also seemed to fit. "I think you're right."

"Wow, an actual flashback. That's so cool," Holly mused.

Cool wasn't the word Victoria would use. She'd been terrified. Worried that Holly was in the midst of a stroke or a heart attack. That she'd have to somehow direct the emergency services through a maze of corridors to the storage unit where her girlfriend had set up some elaborate war room.

Now that she knew it was a memory, other concerns surfaced instead. Was this the start of Holly's memories rolling back in? The familiar dread reasserted its presence.

"Please, come home," she requested.

"I'm fine," Holly reassured her, reaching out for her hand and holding it tightly.

Victoria knew that arguing was pointless, so she looked away so that Holly wouldn't see the traces of tears in her eyes. Holly must have caught sight of them as she found herself enveloped in a hug mere moments later.

"I'm fine, and we're going to be fine, I promise," Holly whispered in her ear.

"I'm going to quit *Arrival*," Victoria said, the thought entering her mouth and being vocalised almost immediately afterwards.

"No, you're not," Holly said, squeezing her.

"I am. Tomorrow morning, first thing. Or Monday. I'll do it Monday."

"You love *Arrival*, you're an industry leader. What would happen if you left? What would you do every day?" Holly released her hold, stood up, and reached a hand down to help pull Victoria up from the floor.

Victoria was so deep in her thoughts that hadn't even realised they were both still on the floor. She took the proffered hand and stood up.

"It might not even make a difference," Holly pointed out. "Then you'd have left for nothing. And someone would still be doing this."

Victoria sighed, pinched the bridge of her nose, and turned away. She paced the small room, infuriated by the situation even more than she had been before.

Which she hadn't thought was at all possible.

"Then what do we do next?" she demanded.

"We keep investigating," Holly explained.

"And if you have another flashback?" Victoria asked. She stopped her pacing. "What if you... you remember something terrible? About me. Because there are plenty of terrible things about me for you to remember. Locked up in that pretty mind of yours."

"Then I'll remember them," Holly said plainly. "And then I'll think about all the wonderful times. I'll remember when I convinced you to go ice skating with Alexia. I'll remember when you baked a cake for Hugo's birthday—"

"It was a disaster." Victoria remembered the catastrophe that had been her first and last foray into the world of cake design.

"It was hilarious. And we all ate it."

Holly took her hands and looked at her affectionately. "I might remember you being mean, but I don't care. It's not like I don't know what you were like. And I have other memories to balance it out. We'll be okay. I promise you."

Victoria held her hands and looked up to her face. She looked deep into the eyes of the woman she loved and hoped desperately that she was right.

CHAPTER TWENTY-TWO

HOLLY SAT on the edge of the bed in her hotel room, her eyes scrunched tightly as she willed the memory to return.

"Come on," she whispered through gritted teeth.

She'd been trying to retrieve more memories, or at least get more of the one she had, for some time to no avail.

The whole thing had been such a shock that she hadn't been able to take it all in at first. She'd never experienced a flashback like it. It completely took her by surprise that her brain had hidden something so personal and so vivid just beyond her reach. Now she wanted it back, as well as whatever other secrets it held on to.

But she couldn't recreate it, and that frustrated her deeply.

She clung to the vague memory, which was already fading from her recollection like a half-remembered dream. Victoria had looked so imposing, towering above her, but also damned sexy in the figure-hugging gown. The problem with the hem was the most minor issue Holly had ever seen, but Victoria had huffed and cursed under her breath as

Holly attempted to use her completely inappropriate skill set to provide a quick fix.

She bit her lip as she wondered what had come next. Had Victoria worn the dress regardless? Had she decided to change? Had Holly helped her unzip the tantalisingly tight dress?

Her eyes flew open, and she jumped to her feet.

"No," she reprimanded herself. "No, none of that. Not now."

She walked in front of the window a few times as she calmed her breathing. Thinking about how beautiful Victoria looked both in and out of her fashionable couture was not going to make her feel any better now that they were apart. She needed to focus on the issue at hand.

She pulled the chair out at the desk and sat down in front of her open notebook. Phoebe Wheeler's name was circled. Phoebe had been one of Holly's early suspects. Not because of anything the woman had done, Holly hadn't even met her since the accident, but simply because of her photographic and digital image manipulation skills. Not to mention the fact that Holly's journals indicated that Phoebe had wanted a promotion for years, even eyeing Victoria's role.

A scandal, especially something involving sex, would easily topple anyone from their position. Especially a woman.

Holly sighed and looked at the other leaf of the notebook. She picked up a pen and added a question mark beside Louise's name. Despite having met her that afternoon to hand the key over, Holly still didn't have an accurate reading on Louise.

The conversation had been short and to the point, Louise signing off with a cold "see you never." Holly winced a little when she considered how Louise would feel when Holly and Victoria announced they were back together again. She didn't like Louise, and the feeling was mutual, but she still felt sorry for her being stuck in the middle of their scheme.

Her phone rang, an unknown number on the screen.

"Holly Carter," she answered.

"Carter, it's Jazz."

"Hey, find anything out?"

"You could say that," Jazz replied. "Did you know your girlfriend has an offshore bank account with money she's stolen from *Arrival*?"

Holly stopped breathing and felt her eyes widen. Then she burst out laughing.

"Good one," she said breathlessly.

"I'm being serious," Jazz said. "There's an account with millions stashed away. It's been going on for years. It took some digging, but Victoria Hastings' fingerprints are all over it."

Holly shook her head. "No. No way. Victoria would never, ever steal from anyone. And not from *Arrival*. She doesn't need to."

"I'm just telling you what I found," Jazz said. "Are you *sure* she's not playing you?"

Holly didn't know what to say. The very thought of Victoria stealing money was absolutely preposterous. And lying to her? Even more so. But she trusted Jazz's skills, which meant something huge was going on.

"I trust her," Holly said.

Jazz sighed. "Look, Carter, I don't want to break your hopes and dreams and tell you that Disney princess lifestyles don't exist, but are you really sure? Like one hundred percent sure? You lost your memory; do you really know her?"

Holly hated that she hesitated, but the truth was that she *did* have brain damage and memory issues and maybe she didn't know absolutely everything. She wanted to trust Victoria; she did trust her. But was there a tiny chance that trust was misplaced? She didn't know.

"I…" Holly trailed off. She rubbed at her forehead with her freehand. "I trust her. I do. I really do."

Jazz blew out another breath. "I can look again, but Carter, I don't know what to tell you. There's an account. It has money in it. It came from *Arrival*, and Victoria's fingerprints are all over it."

Holly felt cold at the very thought. "Please, double-check?"

"Sure. But, you know, don't hold your breath," Jazz told her before hanging up.

Holly lowered the phone from her ear and stared straight ahead.

"Shit," she muttered.

CHAPTER TWENTY-THREE

VICTORIA BREEZED INTO HER OFFICE, surprised to see Phoebe Wheeler waiting for her. The photographer was lounging on the sofa, scrolling on her phone.

"Working on a Saturday?" Victoria asked. "Eager to present your ideas?"

"I emailed you some," Phoebe confessed. "I'm actually here about something else."

Victoria put her handbag by the desk and sat down. She looked at the desktop setup of magazines and water that had been laid out by either Claudia or Louise, whoever had drawn the short straw of suddenly working over the weekend.

"'Something else' sounds ominous," Victoria commented.

"It is. Jimmy Cutler is being sued for sexual harassment," Phoebe said. She stood up and walked over to the chair in front of Victoria's desk and sat down again. "Something from the seventies. It always catches up with them eventually."

Victoria rolled her eyes. It seemed that not a week went by without some high-profile man being accused of some form of misconduct. How they'd all managed to get any work done over the years was beyond her. All of them seemed to have been up to something worthy of jail. She shuddered at the thought.

"So, we need to scrap the entire Bermuda shoot segment," Victoria said, realising that she was suddenly in for a number of long days and that her budget for the next issue was about to be stretched beyond recognition.

"I don't think we have time," Phoebe said. "With the models' schedules at this time of year, there's nothing we can do. On top of that, we've already submitted the budget request for the next issue, and it doesn't include a whole new shoot."

Victoria could feel her blood pressure rising. "We need alternatives fast. Is there anything we can repurpose?" She hated to do it, but sometimes it was necessary. On rare occasions, even a magazine as professional as *Arrival* needed to create a story out of nothing.

"I've been looking at some ideas, but I wanted to let you know as soon as possible," Phoebe said.

Victoria buzzed her outer office. "Editorial meeting in one hour. Tell everyone to turn up or empty their desks."

She knew it was asking a lot for the whole team to assemble on a Saturday morning and her threat was flimsy at best, but no one needed to know that.

"Thank you for the heads-up," Victoria addressed Phoebe.

Phoebe stood up. "No problem. I'll go through my archives and see if I have anything that could work."

Victoria nodded, already opening her laptop and accessing her emails. She didn't even notice Phoebe leave. The last-minute change was the last thing she needed.

She decided then and there to rewrite her Letter from the Editor piece; someone had to say something about the filthy men and their handsy ways. She'd give them a piece of her mind they'd not soon forget, as well as congratulate and offer support to the brave women who were working to bring them down.

Victoria was lucky that she'd never personally been victimised by men, but she knew that was simply a matter of managing to be in the right place at the right time. As a woman in business, especially in the fashion industry, she'd heard all too many tales of other women who hadn't been so fortunate.

It made her blood boil.

"Heard about Cutler?"

Victoria jumped at Gideon's sudden presence in her office.

"Yes, I've just been told. Is everyone working this weekend?"

"I came in as soon as I heard. I have a few ideas to plug the gap," he said. He picked up a magazine from her desk and leafed through it. "Have you and Holly resolved things yet?"

Victoria shook her head. "No."

He looked over the top of the magazine. "Really?"

"Is it such a surprise?" she asked.

"Frankly, yes." He put the magazine back. "I know you have strong feelings for each other, I thought this would be a temporary bump in the road. I can't imagine what could pull you apart."

"Well, I don't know what else to say." She turned away, having to smother a smile at his confirmation that he believed them to be a well-suited couple. She wished he'd go and have a conversation with Phoebe and tell her the same.

"I don't want to put my nose where it doesn't belong," he started, "but maybe I should speak to Holly? See if I can get to the bottom of all of this?"

Victoria shrugged. "If you like."

"I would like. I don't like the thought of you two being apart. I had an outfit picked out for the wedding."

She looked at him and raised an eyebrow. "The wedding?"

"I presumed you would get married eventually," he replied. "I don't know a better-suited pair, despite the obvious differences. You two always seemed to work."

Victoria licked her lips. Her eyes darted to the door to her office. She wanted to tell him everything, to come clean and explain the entire ruse, but she didn't know if it was the right thing to do. She didn't know anything anymore.

"Close the door," she told him.

He frowned but did as she asked. Before he'd even had a chance to sit back down, she was wringing her hands in uncertainty.

"Victoria? What is it?"

"It's all a lie," she said, the words almost erupting from her.

"A lie? What's a lie?"

"Our breakup, it's all a lie. We never really broke up at all. It's this stupid plan because of these ridiculous lies and images, and Holly doesn't trust anyone and now I don't trust anyone either. But I have to tell someone or I'm going to lose my mind!"

Gideon raised his hands to calm her down. He leaned across the table and sought to meet her gaze.

"Tell me what's happening," he requested.

She took a deep breath and poured herself half a glass of water, quickly downing it. She told him everything. The images, the war room in the storage unit, Holly's hotel, the suspects, the possibility of it being someone at *Arrival*.

When she was done, she was out of breath and felt a ton weight lift from her shoulders.

"No one knows," she told him firmly. "Not even the children."

Gideon looked stunned. He removed his glasses, plucked the handkerchief out from his suit jacket pocket, and methodically cleaned each lens. His brow furrowed as he took in everything he'd just heard.

"Victoria, I am so sorry that this is happening to you. To you both," he finally said. "And I'm grateful you confided in me, I'm so pleased I have your trust. I understand the need for secrecy. Obviously, my lips are sealed. I'll do whatever I can to help."

"And Holly experienced a flashback." She sat back in her chair.

He looked surprised. "Of?"

"Me. In Paris. After my hem disaster."

"The floor-length Valentino?"

"Yes."

"You looked divine that night, darling."

She smirked. She knew she had, but it was nice to hear the compliment all the same.

"So, the memories are in there," Gideon said. "Or at least some of them are."

She felt the smirk slip away. "Yes, unfortunately." She winced. "I didn't mean that. Of course, I want Holly to have her memories back. I just, I fear them. I fear them so very much."

"Holly adores you. She did before all of this," Gideon told her. "I can understand the instinct to not want her to remember, but I think it will make you both stronger if and when she does remember."

Victoria wasn't so sure.

"Doubt many things," Gideon said, "but don't doubt Holly's love for you."

CHAPTER TWENTY-FOUR

THE KNOCK on the storage room door caused Holly to jump. She looked at her watch and then at the door suspiciously. It was too early in the day to be Victoria, and she'd just barge in anyway.

She picked up her umbrella and edged closer to the door.

"Come in," she called out, holding the umbrella up and silently hoping that Paul Smith made sturdy enough rain protectors to batter assailants.

The roller door clattered up.

"What on *earth* are you doing here?" she demanded.

Hugo took a step into the storage unit.

"What are *you* doing in here?" he countered. He looked around the room in confused fascination. "It's a little CSI in here, Holly."

She closed the roller door behind them and then spun to face him. "How did you find me?"

"I followed you." He pointed at the whiteboard. "Why

is there a list of people who work at *Arrival* on that? What's going on?"

Holly's mind reeled. She couldn't believe she'd been blissfully unaware of the fact that she'd been followed to her secret location by a sixteen-year-old. Her mind was all over the place following the news of the offshore account. Who knew who else could have followed her in?"

"Hugo, you can't be here."

He sat down on what she'd come to think of as Victoria's chair and stared up at her in cocky determination. "I'm not going anywhere until you tell me what's going on. This weird breakup, it doesn't make any sense. Mom's upset, you're upset. No one is angry—I'm a child of divorce, so I know what that looks like. This isn't it. I want to know what's happening."

Holly ran her hand through her hair. This was one of those parental moments she didn't feel quite prepared for. She had to make a decision, without Victoria, about what to tell her son, who was far too clever for his own good.

On the one hand, she wanted to protect him. On the other, he wouldn't fall for any lie she could speedily construct. To be honest, he knew most of the people on the whiteboard better than she did. He could be a good ally to have.

Besides, Holly was the person who had been trying to convince Victoria over the last few months that Hugo should be treated like an adult. Not only was he sixteen, but he was also mature and intelligent.

"Okay, but Alexia can't know," she said, mind quickly made up.

Hugo nodded.

"Promise me," Holly insisted.

He held up his hands. "I promise. I won't tell her a thing, and I'll back up whatever you tell her."

"Where is Alexia, anyway?" Holly asked, suddenly remembering that Hugo was supposed to be taking her to the cinema that evening.

"She's at Jenny's. Don't worry."

Holly snorted a laugh. Everything made her worry lately. She felt guilty that she was about to spread some of that worry to Hugo.

She pulled her own chair over to sit in front of him. She stared at the floor for a moment while she tried to fathom how to explain everything that had happened.

"You can't tell a soul what I'm about to tell you, even your mother," Holly said.

Hugo frowned. His bond with his birth mother was a close one; they shared more with each other than they did with most other people. He sucked in his cheek, giving the request a moment of thought before slowly nodding.

"I received an email from someone anonymously," Holly explained. "It was a manipulated image of your mother and… another woman."

"Oh, gross." Hugo winced.

"Just kissing." Holly held her hands up to calm him down. "Nothing… too graphic."

She quickly explained the whole situation to him, the images, the emails, the knowledge the person had, her visit to see Ashley, and Jazz's involvement. She took a deep breath before she told him about the offshore account, making him promise to not say a word to Victoria about that part, admitting that she'd yet to talk to her about that.

Hugo silently took it all in, and when Holly had finished he blew out a long breath.

"Wow," he said. "First, Mom would never steal money. She's got savings and a property portfolio; she's told me all about it in case anything happens to her. She doesn't need all that money. She already has money, which means someone must be setting her up."

"My thoughts exactly," Holly agreed, "which is why we need to be so careful about who knows what. We don't know if these two things are connected, if the person who wants to break us up is the same person who has created this elaborate offshore account."

"It's all tied to *Arrival*," Hugo said. He nodded his head towards the whiteboard. "Someone there might be stealing money and framing Mom. What that has to do with you, I don't know."

"Me neither, but we only found out about the offshore account because Jazz is really good at their job."

"Is Jazz a man or a woman?" Hugo asked, confused by the lack of gendered pronouns.

"Neither, Jazz is non-binary," Holly replied.

Hugo's eyes widened in understanding. "Oh, right! Cool, I get it now."

"Jazz is also a genius when it comes to computer stuff, so I trust them," Holly added. "But we don't know if the images and the offshore account are connected. We could be looking at two very different disasters."

"Seems weird, though," Hugo said. "Why would someone want you to be mad at Mom?"

Holly stood up and raised her hands in an 'I don't know' gesture. "Your guess is as good as mine."

"I want to help," Hugo said.

Holly chewed her lip. The more heads the better, and Hugo knew more than she did about certain people on the list. He might have knowledge that would be useful. Then again, he was young, and she didn't know if she should get him involved in something that might be dangerous.

But Holly thought he had a right to know, especially considering how it was affecting him and his family.

"Okay," she said eventually. "But you absolutely cannot follow me again. Someone might have followed you, and we can't take the risk that anyone knows we're onto them. The whole reason I left the house is so they think their plan worked."

"I get it. I can be discreet," he said. "For what it's worth, I'm really glad that you didn't break up. I know Mom really loves you. I've never seen her so happy."

Holly's heart swelled with pride. Her lip quivered as tears threatened to spill over.

"I'm happy, too," she confessed, "and I'd like nothing more than to be home with you all. I wish this would go away, that I could solve it and put things right, but every time I look deeper into this, I uncover something more unsavoury."

Hugo stood up and pulled her into a hug. Even in the short amount of time she'd lived in the Hastings' house, he'd grown. Most boys had a growth spurt at twelve years of age, but Hugo had waited until his sixteenth birthday to shoot up. She wrapped her arms around him.

"I'm sorry. I'm a mess," she said.

"You're not," he promised. "Some asshole is messing

with your family. You have every right to be angry. But I'll help you, I swear. We'll figure this out."

She pushed away, knowing that if she stayed in his embrace any longer the tears she had been holding at bay for the last couple of days would finally break free.

"Thanks, Hugo. I'm angry that you followed me, but I'm really glad you're here," she confessed.

He grinned and then pointed at the whiteboard. "Can we start trimming that list?"

She picked up a marker pen and snapped off the cap. "Be my guest."

CHAPTER TWENTY-FIVE

VICTORIA SAT BACK in her chair and shook her head at what she was seeing on the screen.

"How is it possible that we have nothing usable?" she uttered into the silence of her empty office.

She'd spent the entire day combing through the upcoming issue and all of the shoots they had completed to date to see if there was anything that could be moved around. Her entire schedule had tumbled out of the window as the scandal took over everything.

The original problem still required a solution, finding a replacement spread for the next issue. *Arrival* had plenty of material—photoshoots often had images that weren't used and could be recycled into other issues—but threading them together into a theme that worked was tricky. This was especially true as the best images had obviously been used before and the ones left over had been put aside for a reason.

Phoebe had provided Victoria with links to the vast *Arrival* photography database, allowing her to scroll through thousands of images in a complicated network of folders.

Victoria definitely thought she was developing carpal tunnel with the amount of scrolling and clicking she was doing with the trackpad of her laptop.

"Knock knock."

She looked up and her eyes widened. "Steven! I'm sorry, I completely forgot."

He laughed and nodded. "I'd assumed as much. It's seven thirty and still not a peep from you."

Victoria couldn't believe it was that time already. She'd long ago sent the majority of the staff home, advising them that she needed them in the office first thing the following day. She figured that allowing them some of their Saturday evening off was a concession to the fact that she wanted them in on a Sunday morning.

She'd stayed, knowing the children were busy and having not heard from Holly. If she were at home, she'd be working, so she figured she might as well stay in the office.

Steven walked into the office and sat on the edge of her desk. "What disaster has befallen our illustrious magazine this time?"

"A certain male photographer couldn't keep his hands to himself, so we need to remove any trace of him from the upcoming issue. Unfortunately, he worked on a very large spread for us, and we need to plug the gap. With no time to set up anything new due to cost and schedules, we need to find something in the database that we didn't use in the past and pass it off as a fresh, new idea." Victoria continued looking through folder after folder in the thousands upon thousands of images in the database.

"You must hate that," he commented.

"I do," she confirmed. "But it's that, rush through something subpar, or cut the number of pages, which the advertising department has informed me is completely impossible. So, I'm scratching around on the database for something usable."

She closed another pointless folder and let out a sigh. She turned to look at him and reached out to touch his hand. "I'm sorry I forgot about dinner. There's been a lot going on, and then this popped up. I'm afraid time is more precious than usual at the moment."

"It's fine, but you do need to eat dinner, you know," he looked at her sternly.

She rolled her eyes. What was everyone's obsession with making sure she ate? It wasn't as if she were going to wither away at her desk and be blown to ash by the air conditioning.

"I'll get to it later," she promised. She retracted her hand and turned to look back at her laptop screen.

"I'll tell you what," he said. "I'll order something in, and we can share in here. I'll keep to myself. I also have some work to get to. Then we both get to eat, and we've technically had dinner together. You might even be able to carve out a minute or two to actually speak to me."

She didn't reply, knowing full well that his mind was made up. Out of the corner of her eye she could see him get his smartphone out of his pocket and start typing on the screen, presumably searching for food delivery services.

Knowing that her productive evening was soon to come to an end, she hastened her search for something—anything —usable. She backed out of the folder she was in, clicked once too often, and found herself in unfamiliar territory in Phoebe's filing system.

She read the folder names and saw one labelled *Paris Fashion Week*. Curious, she accessed the folder and saw a list of years. She selected the one for two years ago—the year Holly left.

"You don't like Chinese food, do you?" Steven asked.

"It doesn't like me," Victoria clarified.

She leaned a little closer and looked at the dozens of folders: different designer previews, galas, parties, and more. At the bottom she saw a folder marked *Misc.* and opened it up.

Thousands of tiny thumbnails filled the screen, all the images that didn't fit anywhere else. She previewed some of them and saw various shots that were either blurry or framed incorrectly, test shots, and behind-the-scenes images.

Victoria sought out images with Holly in them and tapped the spacebar to make them full size. A smile curled at her lips. It was strange seeing this Holly, this professional assistant that she hardly recognised anymore.

These days Holly was casual clothes and family dinners. Holly was warm, fluffy pyjamas and ridiculous puns that Victoria tried to keep from laughing at. Holly was home.

Holly in these images was someone she recognised but only a small part of the puzzle. She idly wondered when she had fallen in love with Holly. Was there any trace of those feelings all those months ago?

"Italian, or are you dieting? How is the whole of Italy not huge?"

Victoria opened another picture, this one of her and Gideon on the steps of an art gallery where a preview had taken place. She smiled; she liked the cut of Gideon's jacket. She was about to move on to another image when something caught her eye. She pinched the trackpad and enlarged the background.

Steven stood at the top of the steps, a look of indescribable fury on his face. The look was directed at a retreating Holly. She looked distressed, possibly angry; it was difficult to tell with the angle, but Steven looked angrier than Victoria could even imagine. He'd always been so calm and placid, so the image was a shock.

She felt his hand on her shoulder.

"Ah," he said softly. His grip tightened. "I really wish you hadn't seen that."

CHAPTER TWENTY-SIX

Holly hurried down the street, eager to get back to the hotel so she could have a shower. It had been a long day of research and talking to various people, and she was exhausted.

Seeing Hugo had been a surprise, but it seemed to be working out for the best. He'd helped to eliminate some people from her enquiries and reinforced her faith in Victoria that she wasn't secretly stockpiling stolen funds. She chuckled to herself that she had even considered the idea, no matter how briefly.

She itched to call Jazz and ask if they'd found anything else out, but she knew they had other work to be getting on with and didn't want to chase them. Just because this was the number one thing happening in her world didn't mean that was true of others. It was strange to be in the midst of an all-consuming drama and aware that other people, the ones strolling around her on the sidewalk now, were just experiencing a normal Saturday evening.

Her phone rang, and she eagerly pulled it out of her

bag, hoping that thinking of Jazz had caused them to call. She frowned when she saw Hugo's name on the screen.

"Hi Hugo," she answered.

"Mom's missing," he said without preamble.

She stopped dead in the middle of the busy sidewalk. The words echoed a couple of times in her mind as she hoped that she'd misunderstood them in some way. Surely, he hadn't said what she thought he'd said?

"What do you mean?"

"She's not in the office; her driver didn't pick her up. She's not answering her phone." He sounded panicked. "Carina's here with us, but I don't know what to do."

Holly tried to control her frantic heart rate. It was extremely unlike Victoria to go missing. In fact, it was almost impossible for Victoria to go missing. There were too many people around her for that to happen. Assistants, drivers, housekeepers, and more.

"You called the office?"

"Yeah, I even called the front desk. They said that she swiped out two hours ago, but the driver said she never called. The cars are in the garage. She's just gone."

Holly snapped to attention, strode towards the road, and raised her hand to wave down a taxi. The fear in Hugo's usually strong voice was sending her immediately into mom mode.

"I'm getting a taxi right now. I'll be with you in under twenty minutes. Don't open the door to anyone. Okay?"

She heard his sigh of relief. "Okay," he promised.

She hung up the call and instantly called Victoria's cell phone. She held it to her ear with one hand, the other frantically waving at taxis. Eventually one stopped; she climbed in and gave the address of the townhouse.

The call went through to voicemail. She hung up and then called Victoria's office line, hoping that there had been some confusion and that she was just working late. Maybe her phone was on silent and Hugo had made a mistake when calling the office. Any excuse would do.

As the dial tone kept ringing, she realised that she was living on false hope. She hung up the call and stared at the back of the driver's headrest.

It's my fault, she thought.

She swallowed hard. Had she been wrong all along? Should they have just stayed together and weathered the storm?

Her hand shook, and she realised she had no idea what to do next. Suddenly, her war room and her whiteboards of suspects paled in significance as the reality of the situation hit home.

"Excuse me?" She leaned forward. "Could you drive a little faster? My kids need me."

Holly ran up the steps to the townhouse, slid her spare key into the lock, and rushed through the door. She barely had time to close it again before Alexia and Hugo appeared from the kitchen. Alexia raced into her arms, Hugo not that far behind her.

Holly held them tightly. "Anything?"

"Nothing," Hugo said.

"Holly? What's happening?" Alexia asked, her voice

suddenly sounding so much younger. "Where's Mom? Are you staying here tonight? You have to stay. Please!"

"I'm not going anywhere, I promise," Holly told her firmly.

Alexia responded by tightening her grip around Holly's middle.

"Do we call the police?" Hugo said softly into Holly's ear, trying to keep his concern hidden from his sister.

"Maybe," Holly said, equally quietly. "Though it is a little soon."

Carina coughed to attract Holly's attention. She carefully extracted herself from Alexia and Hugo's grip and walked over to Carina and took her hands.

"She never called to say when she would be back," Carina explained. "I prepared dinner and the children started to call her, but nothing."

Holly realised that all three of them were looking to her for leadership, and she suddenly felt the pressure of that role. She didn't know what to do; for all she knew her actions had put Victoria in danger to start with.

She tried to put herself in Victoria's shoes and thought about what she would do. Her first reaction would be to not panic; the second would be to ensure the children were safe.

She turned around and addressed them both. "Go upstairs and pack an overnight bag."

Hugo looked like he was about to argue.

"Now," she said, channelling as much of Victoria Hastings as she could. She needed people to do as she said and not question her. Not now.

It worked. He nodded and gestured for Alexia to go up

the stairs as well. Once they were safely out of sight, Holly turned to Carina.

"Long story short, we didn't break up," she started to explain.

"I know." Carina nodded.

Holly blinked. "She told you?"

"No, I just know."

It made sense that someone who had worked in the Hastings family home for so long would know Victoria well. This was a relief because it meant saving time she didn't feel she had.

"Okay, well, I don't know what's going on, but there's something happening at *Arrival*. And now that Victoria's vanished, I don't know how safe it is here. I'm going to ask the kids to go to Gideon's. I trust him, and I'm running out of people to trust."

Carina nodded quickly. "He is a good man."

Holly smiled. "I think so, too. You should get home. Thank you for staying with the kids. I'll let you know as soon as I know anything."

Carina put her hand on Holly's shoulder and squeezed. "She will be fine. She is a strong woman."

Before Holly could reply, Carina turned to go and gather her things.

Holly sucked in a deep breath and called Gideon. Thankfully he answered quickly.

"Ah, I've been meaning to call you," he greeted.

"Do you know where Victoria is?" she asked.

"No, should I?"

"She's missing."

"What do you mean by missing?" he asked, all traces of

his usual humour gone.

"Not at the office, not at home. Her driver hasn't seen her. Look, Gideon, I need to explain something—"

"You didn't split up, it was a ruse, I know."

"Did you guess, too?" Holly asked, exasperated that apparently she'd been staying at a hotel for no reason.

"No, she told me this morning. I'm not supposed to tell you that I know, but I think we're beyond that now. Have you called the police?"

"Not yet. I don't know if they'll listen—it's only been a couple of hours—but first I wanted to get the kids sorted out. Is there any chance they can stay with you? Just for tonight. Until I get someth—"

"Of course, I'm happy to have them here."

Holly sagged in relief. Knowing that the children would be somewhere safe was an enormous load off her shoulders.

"Thank you," she breathed. "I'll get a driver to bring them over. Hugo knows what's happening, but Alexia doesn't. They've eaten and, um—" She ran her fingers through her hair, wondering what else she needed to tell him.

"Holly, don't worry. I babysat them when they were kids. Hugo's sixteen. It'll be fine," Gideon reminded her. "Just focus on Victoria."

"I will," she promised. Not that she knew what she was going to do next. Everything had hit her like a bolt from the blue, and now she was scrambling to figure out how to react. She needed to calm the rising panic from inside her and think logically. Once she knew the kids were safe, Victoria needed her, and Holly was determined to find her and bring her home safely.

CHAPTER TWENTY-SEVEN

VICTORIA NEVER THOUGHT she'd miss the drab, poorly lit storage room, but the basement she found herself in was far worse. It was damp, lit by one tiny bulb that swung perilously every time Steven passed it as he paced. The chair she had been forced to sit on was undeniably filthy, with no clean towel to protect her couture this time.

Despite her misgivings about her surroundings, she remained quiet. She knew that speaking up was only going to inflame an already tense situation.

Steven was unrecognisable. That frightened her the most.

His removing a knife from his jacket pocket and leading her from her office into his car took a strange backseat in comparison to the knowledge that the man she'd known for years was a façade.

The kind smile, the light-hearted jokes, the happy disposition were all gone. Now there was a man powered by pure rage as he muttered to himself and stormed around the small basement room as he seemingly wondered what to do next.

She'd gone along with everything he'd said. Handed over her phone, left the office, got into his car, allowed her wrists to be tied, and followed him down to the basement of a house in Brooklyn.

She had no idea where they were. All she knew was that the neighbourhood was run-down. She wouldn't be surprised if the neighbouring properties were empty, a fact that filled her with more dread.

She sat still with her wrists tied together. She was strangely thankful that was all it was, well aware that he could have bound her to the chair. He'd not taken the time to blindfold or gag her. She didn't know if that was because he was ill prepared or because some form of fondness for her still lingered within him.

She swallowed back every sentence that came to mind. Further aggravating Steven was not a sensible choice right now. The best course of action was to sit and wait for him to speak.

Every minute that passed was another minute closer to her being missed. Eventually, someone would put the ball in motion to find her. She just hoped the children were safe, hoped that Steven was working alone.

"You had to ruin everything, didn't you?" Steven suddenly stopped pacing and turned to stare at her, fury in his eyes.

She remained absolutely silent, not wishing to upset him further.

"Victoria Hastings, the woman who goes through assistants like most of us do hot meals. All the same, vapid little girls who just wanted to further their careers. Not a brain cell among them. Until her."

Victoria tried to remain as neutral as possible as she attempted to figure out what was happening: how her best friend of years had suddenly turned into a monster, what had happened in Paris, and why he was so angry at Holly.

"Not only did you have to keep the girl who couldn't be blackmailed or bribed, you then had to *fall* for her. I got rid of her once, but of course she came back like a bad penny, walking around the city like a walking, talking time bomb," he ranted. "Was I supposed to just wait for her to remember?"

Victoria felt a lump in her throat. Holly had been right. This was related to Paris. Not only that, Holly knew something. Or had done.

"I just needed another three months, but you couldn't let me have that, could you?" He turned around and kicked a stack of empty paint cans. They crashed into the wall.

"I can help you," Victoria said, trying to get him back on side before the violence escalated.

He turned and looked at her again. "You can't help me," he said. "No, the only thing we can do now is bring plans forward. I'm sorry, Victoria. I really am."

Victoria didn't know what he was talking about, but she didn't like the sound of it one bit. She kept her mouth closed and looked down at her shoes. She needed to bide her time, hope that someone knew she was gone, even if she did think it would be impossible for anyone to find her.

Her dark humour reminded her that she now knew who

the culprit was. No more whiteboards and guesswork. It had been Steven all along. The next step was finding out why.

CHAPTER TWENTY-EIGHT

As soon as Hugo, Alexia, and Carina were out of the house, Holly slumped against the wall and sank to the floor. A strangled sob escaped her. She had no idea what she was going to do. Victoria was gone, and Holly felt entirely to blame.

Why hadn't she listened to Victoria? They could have stayed together and hired extra security, but no, Holly had to play detective and try to figure it out for herself. She was only now discovering just how far out of her depth she was.

Her phone rang. "Hello?" she answered, desperation obvious in her tone.

"Carter? You all right?"

"Jazz? No. No, not really." Holly rubbed at her face and tried to refocus her attention.

"What's going on?" they asked.

"Victoria's gone missing."

"What do you mean?"

"Like, no one knows where she is. It's only been a couple of hours, but this just doesn't happen with Victoria.

She never disappears like this. It's almost impossible with the amount of staff she has surrounding her."

"I'm coming over," Jazz said. They already sounded like they were on the move.

"I'm at the townhouse," Holly said.

"I know." Jazz read off the address. "I pinged your phone."

Holly's eyes widened as an idea came to her. "Can you ping Victoria's phone?" She gripped her mobile like it was a lifeline.

"Doing it now," Jazz replied.

Holly could hear the sound of typing and then a sigh.

"It's switched off," Jazz said. "The last known location is *Arrival*. That's kind of why I was calling you. It'll be easier for me to show you in person. I'll be there soon."

Jazz hung up, and Holly let out a frustrated sigh. She didn't have time for Jazz to arrive and show her something; she needed to take action now.

If she had any idea what kind of action that should be, she'd be doing it.

"I'm useless," she said out loud. "Completely useless."

She walked over to another table in the hallway and snatched up a picture frame. It was a black and white image of Victoria and Holly in Central Park. Alexia had taken the photo on her phone while they weren't looking. It was one of Holly's favourite images. Holly was looking up at the sky, and Victoria was looking at her as if no one was watching. They both looked happy.

Holly knew that her relationship with Victoria was a blessing, she knew she was deliriously happy and luckier than most, but it was only now that it was at risk that she realised how important Victoria was to her. She didn't know if she could go on without Victoria in her life.

She heard scratching on the floor and turned to see Izzy walk into the hallway.

"Aw, I forgot about you," Holly said. She crouched down and held out her hands for Izzy to come to her. When the big Newfoundland got to her, she wrapped her in a hug. "We'll get her back, girl. I promise."

Holly sat on the floor, one arm draped around Izzy, and started making phone calls. She tried Victoria again, as well as a couple of departments in the building, just in case. Building security at *Arrival* refused to speak to her, and Holly didn't want to raise the alarm just yet. She knew this kind of thing would hit the press very quickly if she wasn't careful.

She didn't know how much time had passed when there was a knock on the front door. Holly looked up. Izzy looked up. Then, they looked at each other apprehensively.

"Come on, Izzy," Holly said as she stood.

They both approached the door, and Holly tentatively opened it.

Jazz stood on the doorstep, eating an apple. "Hey, Carter. Nice dog." They barged their way in. "No news?"

"No. Nothing." Holly closed the door again.

"I did some digging," Jazz said. They looked around the hallway. "Wow, this place is huge. Where can I set up?"

Holly pointed towards the kitchen. They both walked in, Jazz making a beeline for the table and taking various laptops and cables out of their bag.

"Drink?" Holly asked. She felt wired but knew she

needed something in her stomach if she was going to be any good to anyone that evening.

"Sure, coffee's good," Jazz said.

Holly started setting up the coffee machine, looking at Jazz to indicate she was listening to whatever they had to say.

"I did some digging," Jazz repeated, "and I caught something. Tiny little thing, but it got me thinking. Anyway, it led to other little things and before I knew it, I'd come across something really big."

Holly hadn't seen Jazz so excited about something before. Whatever they had managed to uncover was obviously very big news. Holly just hoped it didn't implicate Victoria in any further crimes. She couldn't stomach the idea of Jazz finding apparent concrete evidence that Victoria was in fact a distant relation of Bonnie and Clyde.

"Victoria didn't set up the account," Jazz announced.

Holly let out a sigh of relief. It was the first good news she'd heard in a while.

"It's a really sophisticated plot," Jazz continued, "but there's a big issue."

Holly leaned on the countertop. "I don't know if I can cope with any more big issues today, Jazz."

"The money is gone." Jazz sat down and opened the lid of a laptop. "This evening, it all vanished. And I can't track it."

"How much are we talking about here?" Holly asked.

"Nineteen million dollars, give or take."

Holly blinked a couple of times. "How much?"

"This account has been siphoning money for years. Big amounts, small amounts, for years. It adds up." Jazz typed something on the keyboard. "If I still thought that Victoria had opened the account and found out now that she's gone missing, I'd think she was on the run."

Holly groaned and flopped onto the countertop.

"Exactly," Jazz agreed. "Whoever is doing this is very clever. Diabolical, but clever."

Holly stood up, walked over to the table, and flopped into a chair. "Let me get this straight. There's been an account set up at *Arrival* for years, and it looks like Victoria set it up. Money has been transferred into it for years. This evening it all vanished, at the same time Victoria vanished."

"You got it."

"But you know Victoria didn't set up the account?" Holly asked hopefully.

"Well, I can tell that it wasn't her. Unless she's a computer genius and she's playing us all," Jazz said.

Holly thought back to the evening when she taught Victoria how send a direct message on Twitter. No one could accuse her of being a computer genius. She was barely proficient.

"So, you don't have any evidence, you just know it's too sophisticated for her?" she guessed.

"Exactly. It wouldn't stand up in court, but I can safely guess that she didn't do this. But whoever did…"

Holly felt a shiver run up her spine at the thought of the person who was carrying out such an enormous scam. Nineteen million dollars was a lot of money. Money worth killing for.

"She might be dead," she whispered. Suddenly she was struggling to breathe. The thought that Victoria had been killed so that some faceless criminal could have their money was more than she could stand.

Jazz stood up and put their arms around her. "Hey, Carter. It's going to be okay. We'll figure this out. We just need to follow the trail. Everyone leaves a trail. You're a journalist, you know that."

Holly took a few deep breaths and tried to get herself together. Jazz was right. She needed to compose herself or she'd be no good to anyone. She nodded to indicate she was okay and sat up a little taller. She wiped the tears away from her cheeks.

"We need to know when she left *Arrival,* and what she was doing before she left. There might be a clue," Holly said. "We have to go to the office."

Jazz sat down and shook their head. "No, we have everything we need here." They cracked their knuckles before dancing their fingertips over the keyboard.

Holly dragged her chair around so she could see the screen. Lines and lines of code appeared and disappeared with blistering speed. Suddenly, the screen flashed, and then a desktop with the *Arrival* background appeared on the screen.

"Is that…" Holly trailed off.

"Victoria's computer. We can see what she was doing, emails, everything," Jazz explained.

More lines of code came up, and emails started to pop open.

"All work crap," Jazz commented, boredom clear in their tone.

Documents and images opened and closed, and Holly struggled to keep up with everything she was seeing. It was a glimpse into Victoria's day but at high speed.

"There's nothing here," Jazz complained.

"Wait." Holly pointed at the screen. "Go back. There were pictures of Paris when I was there. Why was she looking at them?"

"Reminiscing?" Jazz guessed.

"Not her style. Not at work." Holly leaned in closer. "There's something here. I can feel it."

Jazz pressed some more buttons and let the timeline run at normal speed. Holly watched as the cursor ambled around the screen, clicking images and folders. She didn't know why, but she knew there was something there. It wasn't Victoria's normal work; it seemed out of place.

"You look hot with long hair," Jazz commented.

"Thanks," Holly said.

"You're okay now," Jazz added quickly. "Not that I'm coming onto you."

"Yeah. I get it, thanks, Jazz." Holly narrowed her eyes at the screen. "There. She's looking at that image far longer than the others. Can we zoom in?"

Jazz typed something, and the image filled the screen.

"It's her and some guy."

"That's Gideon," Holly said.

"There's you in the background. You look pissed." Jazz pointed at the corner of the image.

Holly furrowed her brow. "I don't remember this at all."

"Well, you look like you want to murder someone."

"I do," Holly agreed.

"Who's the guy?" They indicated a figure just within the frame.

Holly cocked her head to the side. "I… don't remember. He seems familiar, but I'm not sure."

The image flashed, and the desktop vanished.

"That was the last thing she looked at before she turned the computer off." Jazz turned to look at Holly. "Seems weird, right?"

"Very," Holly agreed.

She knew she'd seen the man before, but she couldn't quite place him. She bit her lip and tried to remember where she'd seen him. Nothing was coming to her, and she knew stress was playing a big part in that.

She cursed her broken memory and willed herself to relax, hoping that injecting some calm energy into the moment would help her capture the fleeting recognition and put a name to the furious face. She closed her eyes and took a deep, calming breath.

It was then that the doorbell sounded.

They both turned around and looked towards the hallway.

"Expecting company?" Jazz asked.

CHAPTER TWENTY-NINE

Holly opened the door and winced at who she found on the other side.

"What the hell are you doing here?" Louise demanded, shouldering past Holly and into the hallway. "I'm calling the police. You just can't take no for an answer, can you? Honestly, she kicked you out, Holly. Take a hint." She pulled her phone out of her coat pocket.

Holly easily pulled the phone out of Louise's hand and held it out of reach. "Whoa, hold on," Holly said. "I can explain."

"Who's this?" Jazz asked, exiting the kitchen and looking at Louise who was now jumping in an attempt to grab her phone from Holly's hand.

"Who are you?" Louise retaliated, stopping her battle for the device and smoothing her clothes to make herself appear a little more presentable and a little less deranged.

Jazz smiled at the irate woman and then looked at Holly. "Who's this?" they repeated.

"Louise, Victoria's first assistant," Holly explained.

Louise looked between Holly and Jazz in exasperation. "Can someone please tell me what's going on?"

"Victoria and I didn't break up," Holly said. "It was an act to try to flush out someone who sent me anonymous emails and photoshopped images of Victoria in compromising situations."

Louise's jaw dropped open, and she stared at Holly in shock. Holly knew that Louise wouldn't take the news well; for one, she was thoroughly enjoying her role in ejecting Holly from Victoria's life.

"Jazz is a computer specialist who is helping me figure out who sent the emails," she added.

Louise punched Holly in the arm.

"Ow! What was that for?" Holly demanded, rubbing her arm.

"Why didn't you tell me? I could have helped!" Louise said, anger in her voice.

"You were a suspect," Jazz added unhelpfully.

Holly cast them a look, but Jazz ignored her and continued to look at Louise with a lopsided grin.

Oh great, Holly thought, knowing that look all too well. She'd seen Jazz crush on women once or twice before. She didn't need to think about Jazz and Louise together.

"I was a *suspect*?" Louise rounded on Holly again.

Holly raised her hands in defence. "*Everyone* was a suspect," she corrected, tossing another look at Jazz, pleading with them to shut up.

"But you were quite high on the list," Jazz added unhelpfully. "Being so close to Victoria and everything."

"Where is she, anyway?" Louise asked. "I need to drop off this USB stick. She's going to kill me. I thought I gave it to her, but when I got home, I realised it was still plugged into my laptop. I rushed over here."

Holly bit her lip and shook her head sadly. Any residual possibility that Louise was involved was now surely gone. She was innocent—and as useless as Holly was.

"She's missing," Holly said.

Louise stared at Holly for a beat before she held out her hand. "Give me my phone. Now. I'm calling the police."

"We can't call the police," Holly said, keeping the phone away from her.

"Victoria Hastings is missing," Louise said slowly, as if Holly were an idiot. "One of the wealthiest women in New York. We don't wait to tell the police. There's no twenty-four-hour rule when it's Victoria."

Jazz took a step forward. "It's not that simple."

Louise rounded on Jazz, put her hands on her hips, and stared them down. "Oh, really? Why not?"

"Because the police will think she's been embezzling from *Arrival* and that she's on the run," Jazz explained.

Louise blinked a few times, then took a step away from Jazz and turned to Holly again. "What is this crazy person on about?" Louise asked.

"I think we need to get you caught up on everything," Holly suggested. "Jazz, can you get everything up on your laptop so we can show Louise everything from the beginning?"

"Sure." Jazz turned on their heel and walked back into the kitchen.

"Where did you find her?" Louise asked with interest.

"Them," Holly corrected.

Louise's brow knitted together in confusion. "What?"

"Jazz is non-binary. They prefer to be known as them," Holly explained.

Louise's eyes widened. "Fascinating," she drawled. "Once we find Victoria, I need to know everything."

"That's Steven Goodfellow," Louise said as she clutched a mug of hot coffee in her hands. "Odious little creep. Victoria dated him once."

"What?" Holly asked, surprised at the revelation.

"Oh, it was ages ago. Didn't last long from what I heard." Louise leaned a little closer and looked at the photograph on Jazz's laptop screen. "He's furious. And you're not exactly spreading sunshine smiles either. Not like you at all, Holly."

Holly's mind swam with the new information. Steven was Victoria's ex? She had clearly argued with him in Paris. There was something else; he looked so familiar.

"Does he still look like that?" she asked Louise.

"No, he's grown his hair out a little and has a little more stubble." Louise lifted her phone from the table. She'd only been allowed the return of the device after she faithfully promised not to call the police. She pressed a few buttons and then showed the screen to Holly.

"Oh! Yes, I saw him! Just a couple of days ago in the elevator at *Arrival*," Holly said. "He was very friendly."

Jazz stopped staring at Louise to turn and look at Holly. "Well, that's weird."

Louise quickly nodded in agreement. "Yes, because this picture was taken on your last day at *Arrival*. Victoria is going to the Black and White preview here. If I remember her schedule correctly, you later attended the Paul Smith preview with her, and it was soon after that that you vanished."

Holly realised that the car journey to the Paul Smith preview must have been where she finally built up her courage to tell Victoria that she had feelings for her, only to be shot down.

"So, this was probably the last time Steven saw you, until the other day in the elevator," Louise finished. "So, for him to be very friendly, after this was the last time he saw you, is very weird."

"Very weird," Jazz agreed.

Louise turned to raise an accusing finger at Jazz. "I want you to know that I'm not happy about you hacking my boss's computer."

Jazz grinned and leaned back on their chair. "Want me to hack yours instead?"

Louise sighed and rolled her eyes. "No. That's not the point."

Jazz pulled the laptop closer and typed.

Louise ignored them and turned back to Holly. "Now that I'm not on your stupid list of suspects, may I recommend that you put Steven on there?"

"He is on there," Holly confirmed, "and he is rising to the top of the list. What else do we know about him?"

"Ta-da!" Jazz turned the laptop screen to face them.

Louise looked at it and sighed dramatically. "No."

Jazz frowned. "Yes."

"No," Louise repeated.

"Yes," Jazz argued. "This is your laptop. Trust me."

"No, that's not my desktop. My desktop looks nothing like that. My icons are properly organised, for one." Louise pointed at the haphazard icons that littered the screen. "This, this is the work of a madman."

Jazz turned the screen around. "This is your machine. The asset ID is yours."

Louise let out a tired sigh and opened her bag. She pulled out her laptop and opened the lid.

"This is my machine." She gestured to the immaculate desktop. "A place for everything, and everything in its pla—"

Jazz grabbed the machine, closed the lid, and turned it over.

"Hey," Louise said.

Jazz ignored her, looking at the barcode on the bottom of the machine, and then typing something on their own computer.

Louise took her computer back. "You need to work on your manners."

"What is it, Jazz?" Holly asked.

Jazz looked up, confusion written all over their face. "Every device at *Arrival* has an asset ID. It's assigned to a user so that corporate knows who has what. The asset ID on that laptop, is, well, it's yours."

"Mine?" Holly asked.

"Yours. Which is weird, because your asset ID was deactivated when you didn't come back from Paris. But it's here." Jazz pointed at the laptop that Louse held in her hands.

"So, that was my laptop in Paris?" Holly confirmed.

Louise put the laptop on the desk and stared at it in

confusion. "How on earth do I have Holly's laptop? It was filed as missing when she left." She regarded Jazz suspiciously before she leaned in close to Holly. "Are you sure this person is a computer expert?"

"Hey," Jazz said. "It's not my fault *Arrival* can't keep their asset IDs updated."

Louise continued to look at Holly, her tone wondering if they should really be pinning everything they knew on Jazz.

"I trust Jazz," Holly said.

Louise let out a breath and tapped her fingers on the device, deep in thought.

Holly stood up and started to pace the kitchen. So far, they were no closer to finding Victoria. If anything, she just had more questions.

"Wait a minute," Louise said. She sat up straight and looked from Jazz to Holly. "My laptop started acting up not long after Victoria got back from Paris. I remember it because she was an absolute beast and my machine was running slow and kept crashing—not something you want when Victoria's on the rampage. I called IT, but they're useless. I went down there and they were running around like headless chickens, so I just took one of the spare ones from the hot-desking shelf."

Holly crossed the room, took the laptop from Louise's hands, and stared at it in confusion. "So, this *is* my laptop?"

Holly and Louise looked at Jazz, who was still typing and looking at random lines of code on their screen.

"I think it is, but I'll need to investigate it further to be certain," they replied.

"Which means someone brought my laptop back," Holly said.

"Victoria said all your belongings were gone," Louise explained. "She told me to file your laptop and phone as missing."

Holly felt faint. Louise took the laptop from her hands and gave it to Jazz before gesturing for her to sit down. Someone had taken her laptop, maybe her other belongings. She'd always assumed that she'd gone back to the hotel, packed up her things, got into an accident, and been mugged, but the presence of the laptop meant that couldn't be the case.

"What happened to me?" she breathed.

Louise crouched in front of her and took her hands. "I don't know, but we're going to find out."

Questions about her accident had always swum in the back of her mind, but she'd never dwelled on them too much. It was possible she'd never know the truth, in which case the assumed version of events was enough for her to get on with her life. But that reality had just been torn up, and Holly had never wanted her memories back as much as she did now.

"There's a lot of data on this hard drive," Jazz said, "going back a long way." They'd already plugged Louise's laptop into several devices. "I'm going to see what I can recover."

"You do that. We need to get to *Arrival* to talk to the night security guard. There's a guy there I've... seen a couple of times," Louise said as she stood up. "He'll be able to give us some information, and I trust him to keep things quiet."

Holly took a few breaths to get herself back into a state

where she could function properly. She needed to switch gears and fast. Victoria had to be the priority, even if just thinking about where she could be was giving her heart pain.

"I'll stay here and see what I can find. Call me if you need anything," Jazz said.

"Come on." Louise took Holly by the arm and dragged her from the kitchen. "Let's find Victoria."

CHAPTER THIRTY

VICTORIA WATCHED as Steven tapped away on a laptop he'd brought down to the basement. He'd been at it for a while, his fingers dancing across the keyboard like lightning. She'd always known he'd been techy, but seeing him now she realised it was more than that.

This wasn't simply a man checking his emails or updating his address book; this was a man using multiple systems and browser windows at the same time. He looked confident in his deep concentration, and Victoria realised that whatever she was witnessing was part of whatever dreadful mess she had managed to get caught up in.

Following his outburst, she'd remained silent. It afforded her the opportunity to take in her surroundings. The basement had one door at the top of a flight of stairs that led to the main house. There were no other doors and no windows. She suspected that someone was in the house if the occasional creak of floorboards was anything to go by.

She had no idea of the time, but her internal clock told her it was probably around ten in the evening, which meant that surely the alarm had been raised about her disappearance. Hugo would probably call Holly, which meant she was on the case.

Victoria was glad that Holly's journalistic expertise and general perseverance would be helping with the search, but she also loathed the idea that Holly was no doubt fretting about her. She wished she could somehow reach out to her and tell her that she was okay. At least for now.

The thought of Holly being worried caused Victoria's anger to spike. How dare Steven do this, not only to her but also to her family? How dare he lie to her for years, and how dare he hold her prisoner in this filthy basement?

"Is this likely to take much longer?" she asked haughtily.

He looked over the top of his laptop at her, his eyes narrowing.

"You know, I've always hated your attitude, Victoria."

She laughed. "Well, you never said anything, darling. If you'd complained, maybe I'd have changed for you. Seeing as we were supposedly such great friends."

He smiled, a sickly-sweet grin. "No. As much as I hated your attitude, I put up with it so that you would trust me. And sign whatever I put in front of you."

"This is about some papers I signed?" She couldn't believe that all of this ridiculous drama was over some sheets of paper and splotches of ink. What could she have possibly signed to warrant this?

He was right: she did sign whatever was asked of her. If she read every document she was asked to sign, then she wouldn't have a second of time to do any actual work.

Steven had returned his attention to his laptop. She searched her mind, wondering what on earth she had signed. If all of this really was about her signature, then she wanted to know what, precisely, she'd put her name to.

"Go on," she encouraged him. "Tell me what I signed if you're so damned pleased with yourself."

He looked at her again and let out a sigh, presumably still annoyed by her apparent attitude. He stood up and ambled over to her, a cocky grin spreading across his face. He crouched in front of her.

"You know, if you asked me that two hours ago, I wouldn't have said a thing, but now I'm finally free of you. I don't need to worry about keeping you sweet anymore. You see, while you've been focused on models and dresses and all that bullshit, I've been moving money from *Arrival* into a private account."

He stood up and smiled widely, seemingly enjoying the shock on her face.

"Years, Victoria. That's how long this has been going on. At first it was a little here, a little there. Tiny amounts. But then I met someone who helped me move it into the big leagues. They dealt with the technical side of things, and I just kept putting pieces of paper in front of you."

He mimed a signature in the air.

"And the best thing? Everything points to you," he explained. "They'll never find the money now—it's all been scattered—but the paper trail leads squarely back to you."

Her heart pounded at the realisation that one of her oldest friends was in fact her biggest enemy. He'd toyed with her for years in order to gain her trust and make her do his bidding. She'd allowed him to defraud *Arrival*, which felt like stealing money from her children. She couldn't believe she'd been so stupid.

"It's always been the plan to frame you, Victoria. A repayment for having to put up with you for so long. And you make such a pretty scapegoat."

The fact that Steven was so happy to tell her his plan filled Victoria was dread. It meant that, in his mind, she wasn't getting out of there. She wondered how much more he was willing to spill. If she was going to die anyway, she wanted all of the answers, and Steven seemed more than happy to showboat.

"What has all of this got to do with Holly?"

The smile vanished from his face. "Dear, sweet Holly." He shook his head in annoyance. "I suppose I might as well tell you. What does it matter now?"

Victoria didn't say anything in response to the confirmation that this was probably one of the final conversations she was ever going to have. If he was willing to speak, she'd let him.

"Holly overheard a very sensitive phone call," he explained.

She resisted the urge to roll her eyes. He was always a bit of an idiot. She could just imagine him taking a telephone call about his illegal activity in a public place.

"And she couldn't be convinced that she hadn't heard what she thought she heard."

"You mean she couldn't be bribed," Victoria corrected.

He lifted a shoulder with indifference. "She had to be stopped. I made another call to my business partners, and they said they'd deal with her."

Cold washed over Victoria.

She'd always naturally assumed that Holly's accident had been just that—an accident, a terrible event that could have taken her life but luckily had left her with scars and memory loss. Now she was hearing indisputable proof that it wasn't. Not only that, but that Steven was involved. And by extension, herself.

"Don't look so shocked," he told her. "People have done far worse things."

She felt sick to her stomach.

"Of course, the idiot they sent didn't quite manage to finish the job. He reported back that she was dead. It wasn't until much later that we found out she was alive but had no memories. Can you imagine our luck, Victoria? What are the odds of that? It was like a lottery win. The one person who could point a finger at us couldn't even remember how to feed herself."

His glee caused anger to rise within her again, and it took all her strength to sit passively in the chair. He'd sent someone to murder Holly. His only reservation was the fact that the job hadn't been correctly carried out.

"I got rid of her stuff, wiped her devices, and we all agreed that she'd just had enough of you. Perfectly believable that a bright, young woman with her whole life ahead of her would choose to walk away from you. People wondered what took her so long, so you even made that easy for us."

Victoria sat ramrod straight as she imagined all the terrible things she'd do to him if she could. Robbing from *Arrival* was one thing, lying to her was another, but what he'd done to Holly was unforgivable. He'd just admitted to attempted murder, and Victoria felt her blood boil.

He dramatically rolled his eyes. "But then she came back. I was out of the country, so I had no idea until I saw you a few days ago. That was a shocker. We realised we couldn't just kill her off, that would raise suspicions, especially after what happened to her in Paris. She hadn't remembered anything yet, but there was always a risk that she would. So, the obvious choice was to push you apart."

"Which you did," Victoria said.

"And now everyone will believe that you have run off with the money." Steven grinned.

Victoria swallowed hard.

There was the hard confirmation that they planned to kill her. She wished she could see Hugo, Alexia, and Holly one final time, to tell them how much they meant to her. She'd never been good at voicing her feelings, but she'd like one last try.

She wanted to impart every piece of advice she could to Alexia, to tell her to be the brave, strong, independent woman that she knew she would be. She wanted to tell Hugo that she was so immensely proud of him and that she knew his good heart would lead him well.

She wanted to hold Holly in her arms and tell her just how much she loved her. To admit that she'd always had a toe or two out of the relationship in some strange attempt to keep her heart intact should they break up, and to admit how she now knew that was a foolish endeavour. All it did was limit the happiness she could feel, happiness which could have been all-consuming if only she'd allowed it.

If she were given one last chance, she'd explain to Holly what had really happened to her all that time ago in Paris. She knew how desperately her partner sought answers and clarity. It would go some small way to atoning for the part she had played in what happened to Holly, if she could only let her know the truth now.

"Nothing to say?" Steven asked.

"Is there any point in saying anything?"

"I suppose not," he agreed. "If it's any consolation, I'm sorry that it has to end this way."

Victoria didn't believe his false platitudes for one moment. If he did feel any guilt, it was only for himself. Any real man would have shown some kind of shame at embezzling corporate funds and ordering the death of a young woman in his employment.

Steven didn't seem to care about his crimes. He'd obviously long ago convinced himself that he was in the right. There was no sign of the decent man she once thought she knew. He was rotten to the core.

CHAPTER THIRTY-ONE

"I'LL DO THE TALKING," Louise said as they walked into the lobby of the *Arrival* building.

Holly didn't get a chance to reply as Louise marched towards the security officer and greeted him. She blatantly flirted, her voice going up an octave as she greeted him and giggled. Holly wanted to throw up, but she also knew she'd do anything to get the information they sought.

Instead she hung back, not wanting to cramp Louise's style. She looked around the lobby, thinking about Victoria coming and going through it over the years, working alongside people who were stealing from the business, probably trusting them implicitly. It weighed heavily on her that someone would take advantage of Victoria like that.

Suddenly, Louise grabbed her arm and started to drag her outside.

"Okay, she left hours ago with Steven Goodfellow," Louise explained the moment they were on the sidewalk. She got her phone and quickly scrolled through her contacts. "I'll call his secretary."

Holly nodded and got her own phone. "I'll ask Jazz to trace his phone."

They both put their phones to their ears and took a few steps away from each other. Jazz answered quickly and set about trying to trace Steven's phone; it didn't take long to discover that it was switched off and couldn't be traced.

"I'm sorry," Jazz apologised.

"It's okay." Holly pinched the bridge of her nose. She hadn't thought it would be that easy.

"If it's any consolation, I'm rebuilding your hard drive. Whoever deleted it was amateur hour. Some of these documents were created the week you were in Paris."

Holly's heart skipped a beat. Any extra pieces of the puzzle that was that time in her life were going to be gratefully received.

"That's great. Thanks, Jazz."

"I'll call you back when I know more," Jazz said before hanging up.

At the same time, Louise hung up her call and approached Holly. "Greta says that Steven is very chummy with Phoebe Wheeler," Louise explained, an eyebrow raised. "They have been close for a long time."

"Damn," Holly muttered. "Victoria did speak to her and thought she was acting a little suspiciously."

"If you trusted me from the start, I could have told you what a snake that woman was," Louise pointed out.

"I found it a little hard to trust you, considering our history," Holly admitted. "And the fact that you hero-worship Victoria like some teenage fangirl."

Holly didn't have the strength to hold back anymore. If Louise was going to complain about her presence on the suspect list, Holly was going to return fire with all the reasons why she belonged on there.

"Hero worship?" Louise laughed heartily. "She's my boss, and she's one of the most impressive minds in the fashion industry. You might not care about the business, but I do. I'll spend every second I can soaking up knowledge from someone like Victoria. If that's hero worship, then fine!"

"Fine, but you always hated me. Don't deny it!" Holly argued.

"Of course I hated you! You suddenly appeared and upset the delicate balance in the office. Victoria had always relied on me, and then you turned up and I was pushed to one side. You had access to the shoots, the final copy, the layouts, the art department. I was answering the damn phones!"

Realisation dawned on Holly like a light being turned on. Louise wasn't obsessed with Victoria at all; she was obsessed with fashion. She'd always assumed that Louise crushed on Victoria in the same way she had, that they were both vying for her attention. Holly had pushed Louise to one side in her efforts to get closer to Victoria, which had meant that Louise had ended up spending less and less time doing the jobs she liked the most. But that wasn't at all the case. Louise was fascinated by the work but Holly's own crush on Victoria had relegated Louise to the most basic of administrative tasks.

"Louise, I'm so sorry," she said. "I… I was taking my own feelings for Victoria and projecting them onto how you felt about her."

Louise looked up to the sky. "At last, she gets it." She

lowered her gaze back to meet Holly's. "Just because you are head over heels for Victoria doesn't mean we all are. I get that you hate me, but at least I didn't stay at a job I hated just to try to get noticed by my boss."

"You're right," Holly agreed. "At first I needed the job, but I ended up staying because I fell in love with Victoria. That wasn't fair to you and your career. I'm sorry. Really. And for the record, I don't hate you."

Louise looked unconvinced but slightly less angry than she'd been a moment ago. "Well, now that we've sorted that out, should we try to find out where Phoebe Wheeler is?"

Holly shook the cobwebs away and rang Jazz again.

"Shoot, Carter," they answered quickly.

"I need you to see if you can trace a Phoebe Wheeler. She's a photographer at *Arrival*."

"Sure, hold on."

Holly heard the sound of Jazz typing.

"I never trusted Phoebe," Louise claimed.

"Her phone's turned off, too," Jazz said.

"Dammit," Holly muttered. "Her phone is off."

"How about her private number?" Louise asked. She accessed her phone and brought the number up. Holly read the digits to Jazz and listened for the sound of more typing.

"Got it," Jazz said. "It's an address in Brooklyn."

"Does she live in Brooklyn?" Holly asked Louise.

"Please. She wishes," Louise sneered.

"Send me the address, Jazz. We'll check it out."

Louise held up her hand and walked towards the kerb to hail a taxi. For the first time all evening, Holly felt like they had a real lead.

CHAPTER THIRTY-TWO

Victoria resisted the urge to let out a bored breath.

Steven had all but told her that she was soon to be killed, and yet nothing had happened. He'd returned to his laptop and continued to do whatever it was he was doing.

The waiting was driving her mad.

The irritating, useless man was obviously waiting for someone else to come and do the deed. Afraid of getting his hands dirty, she assumed. That thought infuriated Victoria beyond belief. He was nothing but a loud mouth, someone who wanted to gain from his crimes but to not actually be involved in the shadier side of things. The lying and the scheming was one thing, but the fact that he was also useless was quite another.

Am I supposed to wait around for some henchman to come and kill me? Victoria wondered.

She hated waiting for other people, and she hated wasting time. The very idea that she was supposed to sit in a dusty, dank basement and wait for someone to bother to show up and end her life—a life she was actually enjoying immensely for once, thank you very much—was intolerable.

This is madness, she thought to herself. *I'm not going down without a fight.*

CHAPTER THIRTY-THREE

LOUISE MARCHED up the path to the almost derelict house. Holly grabbed her arm and pulled her back, behind an overgrown bush.

"What are you doing?" Holly demanded.

"Knocking on the door," Louise said as if it were absolutely obvious.

"Great plan, Louise, really. We'll just knock and let them know that we're here and that we know they're here, giving away our *only* advantage."

Louise folded her arms. "Fine. What do you suggest we do?"

Holly looked around the dark and overgrown garden. "We need to get closer to the house and try to see inside without letting them know that we are here."

"Fine, fine." Louise shooed her away.

Holly looked around the bush and couldn't see anyone, so she crept towards the house, keeping to the shadows cast over the garden by the trees and bushes. She stared at the dark windows, wondering if anyone was there and able to see her.

Thank goodness Jazz knows where we are, she thought.

They reached the house, and Holly peered through the window. Everything was dark. She looked at Louise and shook her head before indicating that they should move around to the back of the house.

They hugged the wall of the house and continued around the corner. There they could see a flickering light spilling out into the back garden. Holly immediately recognised it as the light of a television. Her heart rate spiked at the knowledge that someone was probably in the house. She crept a little faster around the corner and peeked in through another window.

She saw a television and an old sofa facing it; Phoebe was draped across it with her mobile phone in her hand.

Holly ducked down. "She's in there," she whispered.

Louise gestured for her to move so she look through the window herself. She slowly stood up and took in the view. She tutted and then crouched down again.

"She's playing Candy Crush. She's obsessed." Louise shook her head.

"What do we do?" Holly asked.

"Break in," Louise said; she tilted her head towards the door. "Come on. No time to lose."

Before Holly had the chance to argue, Louise was off and creeping towards the door. She tried the handle and then grinned as the door opened a crack. Holly hurried to catch up.

By the time she arrived at the door, Louise was already through it. Holly wanted to call out to her and tell her to slow down and come up with a plan rather than forging ahead, but Louise was determined and moved like lightning. Holly knew she had to remain silent in order to keep their element of surprise.

She followed Louise through the door and found herself in a kitchen. It was run-down, like the rest of the property, but still usable. Holly noticed a coffee mug on the countertop and saw that it looked recently used.

She turned to indicate the mug to Louise, but Louise was already marching into the sitting room. Holly watched in shock and pleasant surprise as Louise grabbed hold of Phoebe, tossed her phone onto the sofa, and then forced the woman into a headlock.

"What the hell are you doing?" Phoebe demanded, clutching at Louise's arm which was tight around her neck. "Let go!"

"The more you struggle, the tighter I hold on." Louise looked up at Holly. "Self-defence is essential in this city. Don't just stand there; check the other rooms."

Holly quickly looked around the house, which didn't take long—there was only one bedroom and all the other rooms were empty. When she got back to the sitting room, Louise still had Phoebe in a tight grip.

"Where's Victoria?" Louise demanded.

"I don't know what you're talking about," Phoebe said, though it was obviously a lie.

Holly was incensed. She crouched down to meet her eye to eye.

"Where is she?" Holly demanded, venom dripping from her voice. She didn't know what she would do next. She felt like she was capable of things she'd never thought possible.

Phoebe obviously knew something, and Holly would happily claw the truth from her.

"Where?" Holly repeated.

"I'm here."

Holly jumped and spun around.

Victoria stood in the doorway. Her usually perfect hair was slightly askew and there was a thin cut on her forehead, but otherwise she looked fine. Holly rushed to her and gathered her into a hug.

"I thought I'd lost you," she whispered. "I've been so scared."

Victoria patted her back gently. "I'm fine. But we have to call the police."

"That might not be such a good idea," Holly said.

"It's okay. I know about the offshore account and I have all the evidence I need to prove my innocence, but we need to call the police now," Victoria explained, her voice even and calm.

Holly had missed that voice so much. She'd missed her partner, her other half, the person who could be strong when she couldn't.

"I'm on it, Victoria," Louise said, her phone in one hand, her free arm still holding Phoebe in a death grip.

Holly looked at Victoria again, taking in the cut and frowning.

"You're hurt. What happened?"

Victoria cupped her face and kissed her. "I love you," she said with such feeling that Holly felt her breath catch in her chest.

"I love you, too," she said.

"The children?" Victoria asked.

"Safe. With Gideon."

Victoria sagged in relief. She turned her attention back to Louise. "Call for my car and ask my lawyer to meet me at the house as soon as possible. He's about to earn his money."

"On it," Louise said. She started dialling another number, giving Phoebe's neck a little squeeze when she started to fight back.

Victoria looked at Phoebe as if only just seeing her. She nodded her head and smirked. "Ah, yes, that makes sense."

Holly looked behind Victoria to a doorway she hadn't seen before; some steps led down to where she presumed there was a basement. Holly edged around Victoria and looked down the stairs.

"You can go down there if you like," Victoria said. "Give him my regards."

Holly frowned, not knowing what Victoria was talking about. She took a few tentative steps down before crouching to look into the room. There was a chair in the middle of the room; a man was tied to it with the cord of an old lamp, which hung uselessly on the floor.

She recognised him as Steven Goodfellow despite the blood streaming down his nose.

"Holly!" He looked at her pleadingly. "Holly, she's gone crazy. She attacked me, please help!"

Holly continued down the stairs and looked at him suspiciously.

Steven tried to move and gestured to his hands with a nod of his head.

"Untie me. Please, you don't know what she's capable of," he said.

"Darling?" Victoria's voice floated down the stairs. "Please bring the laptop with you when you come back up here."

Holly looked around the room and saw the laptop.

"I've been set up," Steven said the moment her eyes zoned in on the device.

"Yeah, there's a lot of that going around," Holly said.

She looked at the laptop; there was a browser window with multiple tabs open. She looked through them; many were bank accounts all showing recent deposits. One tab was an email account where Steven was halfway through typing his resignation to *Arrival* and claiming he wanted to spend more time with his family.

She closed that email and looked at his outbox. The last message he'd sent was to an email address she didn't recognise informing them that he had Victoria Hastings and requesting advice on how to dispose of her, hoping that they he would be able to hire someone to do the job for him.

Holly looked up at him, fury in her eyes. The monster had framed Victoria and was now requesting that someone come and *murder* her. On top of that he had the audacity to pretend that he was being framed.

"This doesn't look good for you, Mr Goodfellow," she said. She picked up the laptop and walked over to the stairs.

Steven laughed. "You'll regret this."

"Maybe," Holly allowed, "but I think you'll regret this more."

She climbed the stairs and handed the laptop over to Victoria.

"Did you attack him?" she asked.

"I did. Thanks to you and Rambo over there," Victoria said as she tucked the laptop under her arm.

"Why us?"

"Steven heard you walking around outside and then heard the back door open. It was all the distraction I needed. The fool hadn't bothered to tie me up, presumably because I'm a feeble old woman. Unfortunately for him, my Jimmy Choo heel is as tough as any twenty-year-old's."

Holly blinked. "You hit him with your heel?"

"Of course. You don't expect me to punch him like some thug, do you?" Victoria softly patted the laptop. "This will do nicely. I knew that pathetic excuse for a human wouldn't think for a second that I'd be able to overpower him. He was stupid enough to leave all the evidence right here."

"Let me go," Phoebe shouted.

Louise held her firmly in place and looked at Victoria. "Your car is on the way."

"Excellent. Thank you, Louise."

Holly stared at Louise as she effortlessly held Phoebe in the headlock.

"Self-defence training," Victoria explained. "I insisted on it for all staff members a few years ago, prior to Phoebe's time with us. It's essential in this city."

"So I hear," Holly said.

"I'll talk," Phoebe said. "I'll tell you whatever you want to know."

"I think I already know everything," Victoria said. "Any bartering you want to do can be done via the police."

As if on cue, blue lights illuminated the house.

"And here they are now," Victoria said. She handed Holly back the laptop and walked over to the front door.

"Officers," Victoria greeted as she opened the door. "I'll make this quick as I'd really like to get home. I've had a very trying evening."

CHAPTER THIRTY-FOUR

Victoria finally walked out of the dingy house in Brooklyn, Holly's hand firmly in hers. She couldn't believe that it had taken fifteen minutes to explain everything to the dim-witted officers. It wasn't until she called the chief and explained things to him that the wheels of justice started to move a little more smoothly. Suddenly, she was free to go and asked to come to the station in the morning.

Louise had quickly volunteered to stay and ensure everything was in order. Victoria planned to extract an apology from Holly for ever doubting Louise's loyalty.

Once she had properly said hello, of course.

"Miss Hastings," the driver greeted her, holding the back door to the Town Car open for them. "Miss Carter."

"Hello, Graham," Holly greeted him before entering the car.

"Home, as quickly as possible," Victoria instructed with a small grin of thanks for his prompt arrival.

"Yes, Miss Hastings," he agreed before closing the door.

Victoria immediately pressed the button for the privacy screen to rise. The twenty seconds it took felt like an eternity, but the moment it was sealed in place she lifted herself out of her seat and straddled Holly.

Holly was surprised but quickly took hold of her hips. The feeling of being held by the woman she loved allowed her stress levels to lower ever so slightly.

"Let's never be apart again," Victoria said seriously as she clasped Holly's face and stared deep into her eyes. "Never."

"Never," Holly agreed readily.

Victoria lowered her lips to capture Holly's in the kiss she'd wanted to give her since the moment she clapped eyes on her again. She'd been living in a state of terror for a while and hearing the clumping footsteps around the house had convinced her she was about to die.

It was only when Steven looked equally confused by the door opening upstairs that she had realised she had an opportunity. She'd hit him squarely in the nose, and then over the back of the head. She'd have to call Jimmy Choo and commend them on their excellent wedge.

Steven had come towards her, and she'd kneed him hard in the groin, very satisfied when he writhed on the floor in agony. She'd tied him to the chair and gone upstairs to confront her next foe, ready to fight her way out of the situation and high on confidence attained from one man down.

But she'd not needed to. Louise had some woman with terrible split ends in a headlock, and Holly was demanding to know where she was. Propriety and a desire to get out of the house and to safety had stopped her from pressing an extremely passionate kiss to Holly's warm lips. But that was then, and this was now. She felt like she had earned her prize with her patience.

Holly grasped at her, tugging her blouse free from her trousers and placing her hands on the skin she found there. Victoria sighed at the connection. She meant what she had said; they were not going to be parted again.

In fact, she was going to do whatever it took to keep Holly close.

She tore her lips away. "We should call the children."

Holly's eyes were wide and dark. She nodded. "I was going to suggest that," she said huskily, "but then you seemed to have other ideas."

Victoria extracted herself from Holly's lap and took her seat. Holly handed over her phone, and she belatedly remembered that hers was still at the office.

She unlocked the phone and called Gideon.

Holly reached over and took her hand in a tight grasp. She raised the hand and kissed her knuckles.

"Holly, have you heard anything?" Gideon answered.

"It's me," Victoria replied.

"Oh, thank god, you're okay. What happened?"

"I'll explain everything in the morning," Victoria said. "Suffice to say, Steven Goodfellow has been embezzling from *Arrival* for years and using me to do it. There's more to it than that, but he's in police custody now. This will need some major damage control. I'll need you at the house tomorrow morning. Oh, and we'll need to talk about the replacement spread. I had an idea abou—"

Holly squeezed her hand lightly.

"That can wait. Are you okay to keep the children with you tonight? It's late, and there's no sense in moving them now."

"Of course, Alexia fell asleep watching television. I let Hugo clean up my Spotify playlist; he needed a laugh. Do you want to speak to him?"

"Yes, please."

"One moment." She heard shuffling as Gideon went to get Hugo.

She turned her head and looked at Holly again, knowing she was never going to grow tired of seeing the woman by her side.

"Mom?"

"Darling, I'm fine," Victoria said, immediately detecting his worried tone. "Not a hair out of place, just some silliness. I'll explain everything to you tomorrow. I'll have Louise call the school and tell them that you won't be attending tomorrow."

"You're sure you are okay?" he clarified. "And Holly?"

"She's right beside me; we're both fine. Safe and well. Please wake your sister and tell her that you've spoken to us both. Then make sure she goes to bed and gets some sleep. I'll send a car for you both first thing in the morning."

"I love you, Mom," he said, relief evident in his tone.

She'd rip Steven limb from limb for doing this to her family. She'd see to it that he'd rather take a thousand Jimmy Choo wedge blows to the head before even thinking about toying with her loved ones again.

"I love you, too, sweetheart. Both of you, more than I can say." She ended the call and handed the phone back to

Holly. She took a deep breath, closed her eyes, and leaned her head back against the headrest.

Holly squeezed her hand, and they sat in comfortable silence for the remainder of the journey home.

CHAPTER THIRTY-FIVE

Holly put her key into the lock of the front door and let them both in. As she crossed the threshold, Victoria breathed a sigh of relief. She couldn't believe she was finally home.

There had been moments in the basement when she honestly thought she'd never see her family or her home again. This was the first major step in her realising that everything was going to be okay.

She opened her mouth to say something but heard footsteps coming from the kitchen. She grabbed hold of Holly's arm and pulled her behind her, ready to confront whoever had broken into the townhouse while they had been out.

Holly placed a calming hand on her shoulder. "This is Jazz. They've been helping me."

Victoria looked Jazz up and down. She picked up on Holly's use of gender-neutral pronouns and noted Jazz's lightly feminine facial features and androgynous clothing.

"Actually, without Jazz, I wouldn't have found you. They really put everything together for me," Holly continued.

Victoria stuck out a hand. "It's a pleasure to meet you, Jazz. Thank you. I don't think it's an over-exaggeration to say that you saved my life."

Jazz shook her hand. They looked a little in awe, something Victoria was more than used to. "It's fine, it's my pleasure. I've worked with Carter a lot; she's good people."

"She is," Victoria agreed. "The best."

"Is everything okay? Did you find Phoebe?" Jazz asked Holly.

"Steven and Phoebe were working together. They were the ones who had been siphoning money from *Arrival*," Holly explained.

"I'm afraid it goes deeper than that," Victoria said.

She hadn't explained everything to Holly just yet; it wouldn't be an easy conversation to have. The short rest she'd had in the back of the car had rejuvenated her enough to start thinking about how to explain everything she'd learnt.

"Wow," Jazz said. "I saved everything I found on a USB stick; hopefully that will help the police to follow the trail. But, I'd rather you kept my name out of it?"

"Of course," Victoria agreed. "There's no need for you to become too deeply embroiled in this."

"I also found something on your laptop, Carter," Jazz said.

Holly turned to Victoria. "You won't believe this— Louise had my old laptop. The laptop I had in Paris. Somehow it got back to *Arrival* in New York, and then through some weird series of events, Louise's laptop was acting up and IT was being slow as usual. So, she just grabbed a spare one. She's been using it for over two years."

Victoria stared at her in confusion. "Yours?"

"Yes. I don't know how it got back here."

"I think I do," Victoria said. She turned back to Jazz. "You said you found something?"

"Yes. I rebuilt some of the deleted files. A lot of it was work stuff—emails, event planning, table seating, memos— but I did find something that I think you're going to want to see," Jazz said, gesturing for the pair to follow them into the kitchen.

Victoria took Holly's hand, and they walked into the kitchen. Or rather, what was left of her kitchen. The entire table had been taken over by empty used plates, laptops, tablets, and cables.

Jazz sat down and gestured for Holly to look at the screen. "I didn't read them," they said quickly.

Holly took one look at the screen and gasped. "My journals!"

Victoria resisted the urge to look over her shoulder. She knew Holly was private about her journals, and rightfully so. She smiled as she watched Holly scrolling and happily lapping up the new information.

Holly looked at Victoria. "I sometimes typed up my journals when I was travelling, then I printed them out and stuck them in the physical books. This literally covers every-thing that happened up to the day I... the day of the accident."

"I rebuilt as much as I could. I think all of the journal entries you wrote at the time have been recovered," Jazz explained. "They're on this USB." They pointed to the other stick on the table. "The one labelled 'fuzz' is for the police."

Victoria knew that her lawyer wouldn't be happy with a

presumed hacker providing evidence, especially if that hacker wished to remain anonymous. And Michael was on his way.

"Jazz, I think we might have some company soon," Victoria said gently. "My lawyer."

Jazz nodded and quickly started to unplug equipment and throw it into a rucksack.

"We'll be in touch to reimburse you for your time," Victoria explained.

"No need," Jazz said. "I'm glad I could help."

"We'll be in touch to reimburse you for your time," Victoria repeated in a tone not to be argued with.

Jazz swallowed nervously. "Um. Okay."

Victoria tried to keep a neutral expression on her face.

"What?" Holly asked.

Clearly, she failed.

"I'll see myself out," Jazz said as they slipped away.

Victoria licked her lips and looked around the kitchen nervously. How could she tell her girlfriend that her long-ago ex had tried to kill her? She wasn't very good at the most standard of interactions; this was well beyond her capabilities.

"I can hear the cogs in your brain going a thousand miles an hour," Holly said. "What is it?" She stood up and took Victoria's hand in hers. "Whatever it is, it's okay." Victoria blew out a breath and gestured for Holly to sit down again. She dragged another seat over and sat directly in front of her. "Your accident was perpetrated by Steven. He admitted everything to me. He was boasting about how clever he was, typical man."

"He did this to me?" Holly frowned.

"Steven? No, he's a coward. He and whoever he works with on this embezzling scheme hired someone to, well, to kill you."

Holly paled, and she sat back in her chair. "Kill me?"

"Yes. I'm afraid so. You'd found out that he was stealing. He tried to bribe you, but you weren't going to be bought. So, they hired someone to get rid of you. That person didn't finish the job, thank heavens."

Victoria stopped speaking. She could see that Holly was reeling from the news. She gave her a few moments for that to settle before she continued. "Steven found out that you were in the hospital with memory loss, and he took that as a win. He… he left you there and didn't tell anyone. He brought your laptop and your mobile phone back to *Arrival* after wiping them. Everything else, I presume he disposed of."

Victoria realised she was clenching her hand so tightly that she was nearly drawing blood with her nails embedded in her palms.

In many ways she was lucky that she'd been eager to get out of the basement and upstairs to confront whatever new assailant lurked there. If she'd stayed in the basement with Steven, there was a chance she would have killed him.

Her mind tortured her with thoughts of what-ifs. What if, back in Paris, Holly had managed to tell her what she found out? What if Steven had succeeded in his original scheme and Holly had died? What if Holly had never found out about his scheme at all?

No matter which way she looked at it, Holly was an innocent bystander caught up in Steven's money-hungry scheme, and, for that, he needed to pay. Dearly.

But right now, Victoria was solely focused on making sure that Holly weathered the latest storm as best she could.

Holly's mouth opened and closed a few times as she processed what she was hearing.

"I'm so sorry," Victoria said. "What happened to you happened because of me."

Holly's eyes glinted with anger. "Don't ever say that. You aren't to blame for what *he* did to me."

Victoria swallowed, never having seen Holly's fury burst forth like that.

"This was all him," Holly said firmly. "Anyone who worked with you and with him could have been in the line of fire. It just happened to be me."

Victoria opened her mouth to argue but thought better of it. Holly was adamant, and any debate could be saved for another time.

"You need to see a doctor," Holly said, indicating Victoria's forehead.

She stood up and looked in the mirror that hung on the wall. A small cut grazed her hairline above her right eye. She didn't even know when it had happened.

"I'm fine. Hardly worth worrying about," she said.

"I did all of this wrong," Holly said. "We should have stayed together. Playing along just meant you were put in danger."

Victoria put her hand on Holly's shoulder. "It wouldn't have made a difference; Steven wanted us apart. If the images hadn't worked, then he would have tried something else. Whatever happened, we were always heading for this destination. Apparently, his plan was coming to an end soon anyway."

"I know. I thought I'd lost you," Holly whispered, her voice breaking.

Victoria crouched down and caught her gaze. "You're not going to lose me. I'm far too stubborn."

Holly chuckled as some tears trickled down her cheek.

"But I'm going to do something I should have done at the start of all of this," Victoria said. She stood up and snatched her phone from the table. She started to compose a text to Louise. "Starting this evening, we're going to have full-time security at the house, at the office, following you, me, and the children. No arguments."

"No arguments from me," Holly said.

Victoria fired off a text to Louise and then put the phone back on the table. Her stomach growled. Holly frowned and looked at her with concern. "When did you last eat?"

Never mind prison for Steven, Victoria thought. *Just have him admit to Holly Carter that he hasn't eaten for twelve hours.*

"A while ago," she said vaguely.

"I'm making you a sandwich." Holly jumped up and started cleaning the plates away. "If Jazz has left anything to eat in the house."

Victoria wasn't going to argue; a sandwich sounded divine. She hadn't realised how hungry she was until that exact moment.

Louise texted back to say that Steven and Phoebe were in custody. She was on her way to the house with some paperwork, and security was also on the way.

"So, it wasn't Louise," Victoria said triumphantly as Holly pulled a loaf out of the bread bin.

"No." Holly grinned. "It was your ex."

Victoria felt the blush on her cheeks. "Ah, you know."

"Yes, I know." Holly chuckled. "You sure know how to pick them."

Victoria smirked. "I do, don't I? Well, admittedly I didn't know he was committing fraud at the time."

Holly held up a mug. "Coffee? It's going to be a long night."

"Yes, please." She watched as Holly flitted around the kitchen, making food and cleaning things away as if she'd always been there. It seemed inconceivable to think of the house, or her life, without Holly Carter.

"By the way," Holly said, "I had a conversation with Louise, and I apologised."

"Whatever for?"

"For being helplessly in love with you when we worked together and shouldering her to one side so I could spend more time with you." She grabbed some items from the fridge and arranged them on the counter. "I realised that I'd been projecting my own feelings for you onto Louise. She doesn't hero-worship you; she thinks you're a genius and wants to learn from you."

"Well, I am a genius," Victoria agreed.

"And so modest." Holly chuckled.

The doorbell rang. "That will be the lawyer," Victoria said. "And so it begins."

CHAPTER THIRTY-SIX

HOLLY SMOTHERED a yawn behind her hand. It was the very early hours of the morning, and she, two police officers, Michael, Victoria, and Louise all sat in Victoria's office, going through everything that had happened.

Notes were made, questions were asked, clarifications were made. At one point the doorbell rang to announce the presence of a very large man called Keith from the security company. He checked the house from top to bottom with Louise's help and then formulated a plan to keep the house under surveillance.

Holly watched Victoria take the lead during the police questioning. She was so powerful and confident as she handed out instructions and explained in her soft yet authoritative tone what had happened and what she expected to happen next.

It was incredibly sexy, and Holly was getting some insight into what she must have seen in Victoria when she'd worked as her assistant. She could just imagine sitting in meetings and watching the impressive editor dishing out orders in that impossibly soft voice, everyone sitting to attention and waiting for their instructions.

During some of the quieter parts of the early morning, Holly had accessed her newly recovered journals. It was a revelation to finally read what had happened on the trip, from boring day-to-day details right up to the momentous decision to tell Victoria how she felt.

Even though it went terribly and Victoria had harshly turned her away, Holly didn't regret a thing. Taking that brave action had proved to Victoria that her feelings were real, had been real even back then.

There was a line in her journal about Steven Goodfellow, stating that she felt something was going on, but she couldn't be sure what. She'd made a note to investigate some of the things he'd said when she got back to New York.

Steven had been sure that she knew everything, but that couldn't have been further from the truth. Maybe that would have changed with further investigation, but the fact remained that, when Steven had requested that Holly be murdered, she'd not known a thing.

That angered her the most, the pointlessness of it all. And for nothing more than greed.

Steven's more recent plan to pull them apart had backfired tremendously. She and Victoria had grown impossibly closer—to be expected, she guessed, after such a heart-wrenching time—but Holly couldn't possibly think of spending time apart now.

She wanted to know that she could lay her eyes on Victoria any moment she chose to. Victoria's eventual return to *Arrival* would be hard, but she didn't have to worry about that for a couple of days at least. Louise had everything in order, and Gideon would pick up the rest of the slack.

Eventually the police left, having everything they needed to begin proceedings and hold Steven and Phoebe for their crimes. Victoria bade them farewell and then spoke with Michael about what would come next.

Holly left the room and sought out Louise.

"Hey," she said as she found the woman searching for food in the kitchen. "There's cookies in that tin." She pointed to the blue tin on the top shelf.

Louise pulled the tin out of the cupboard. She opened it and grabbed one and put the whole thing in her mouth.

"Don't tell Victoria," she said through a mouthful of cookie.

"I won't." Holly leaned on the countertop. "Louise, you and I need to be friends."

Louise frowned as she chewed.

"I know you didn't like me when we both worked for Victoria, and I understand why now."

"I liked you; you didn't like me," Louise argued, swallowing quickly before picking up another cookie. "You made that very clear."

"Well, I obviously can't remember any of that. But from my journals, I can tell you that I never hated you. Well, we grew to dislike each other, but at the start, I respected you. You were good at your job, and you taught me well."

Louise looked at her suspiciously as she chewed.

"The thing is," Holly said, "despite what you may think, I'm here to stay. I love Victoria, and I'm not going anywhere. I know Victoria depends on you, and I know you like working for her. Even if she is going to push you into an early grave."

Louise smiled. "She probably is," she admitted. "But I don't… *like her* like her or anything. I just respect her."

"I know." Holly nodded.

"I'm willing to start afresh if you are," Louise said.

"I'd like that. A clean slate."

"On one condition."

"Name it." Holly was willing to do almost anything to put an end to hostilities.

"Could you give me Jazz's number?" Louise asked, a hint of colour on her cheeks.

Holly smiled. "Yes! Absolutely." She recalled the way Jazz had stared at Louise and knew that they would be excited at the prospect. "We can double date."

"No," Louise said flatly. "No offence, but I don't need to see you making goo-goo eyes at my boss."

"Don't you like her goo-goo eyes?" Victoria asked as she entered the kitchen.

Louise slid the cookie tin behind the toaster.

"Don't tease her," Holly instructed. "We've just come to a truce; she likes me now."

"I-I've always like you," Louise lied.

Victoria smirked. "Louise, exemplary work today as always. I know I don't say that often."

"Or ever," Holly added.

"Or ever," Victoria agreed. "But well done. I can't adjust your *Arrival* salary, obviously, but I will ensure that you are appropriately compensated for your help tonight."

"You don't need to do that," Louise said.

Victoria gave her an indulgent smile. "Of course, I'll

need a replacement photographer ready for work when I get back in two days. Oh, and Izzy needs to have her nails clipped. And Alexia wants to take up the violin, or the cello, or was it the double bass? Get all three. Tomorrow." She turned on her heel and left the room.

Louise was already on her phone making preparations despite it being the middle of the night. Holly shook her head with a smile on her face. She wasn't about to come in between the strange relationship Victoria and Louise had; it seemed to work for them.

CHAPTER THIRTY-SEVEN

It was nearly five o'clock in the morning when Holly finally slid into bed. She let out a deep, contented sigh.

"I've missed this bed," she said.

Victoria sat at the vanity table, brushing her hair and waiting for her face cream to sink into her skin.

"I should think so," Victoria said, watching her in the reflection. "It's bound to be far superior to whatever straw-filled sack you endured at that motel."

Holly rolled her eyes. "It was a nice hotel," she pointed out.

Victoria hummed rather than issuing the outright denial that she clearly wanted to.

"There is one problem with this bed." Holly propped her head up on her elbow.

Victoria raised a confused eyebrow.

"It's strangely empty," Holly explained, running her hand over the soft sheets.

Victoria smirked. "Well, let's see what we can do about

that." She lowered her hairbrush, gave herself one last look over in the mirror, and then climbed into bed.

Holly shuffled over and snuggled up against her, fitting perfectly into the crook of her shoulder. She wrapped her arm around Victoria's middle. Victoria reached up and switched the lights off. The early morning sun was already peeking through the curtains.

Holly closed her eyes and listened to the soft breathing of her partner.

She wasn't at all tired. Her mind was still a blur of information and further questions. Things weren't settled, but at least they were now safe, and together. The few short days away from Victoria had been a shock to Holly.

She'd obviously known that she was in love with Victoria, but just how in love she was had proved to be a surprise. Not a second had gone by without her thinking about her missing other half.

Holly had always known deep down that she was in this relationship for the long haul. She'd felt that way almost immediately, and every new passing day served to cement those feelings.

Logically, she knew that they hadn't been together long and that they faced a mountain of opposition from people who thought they were mismatched, but that didn't matter. She knew how she felt.

"Are you asleep?" she whispered.

"How could I sleep?" Victoria answered honestly. "A madman just kidnapped me."

Holly wanted to point out that most people would be utterly exhausted after being kidnapped and having found out that one of your nearest and dearest friends had been using you for years. Not to mention everything else that had been going on.

But Victoria wasn't most people.

Holly loosened her grip on Victoria's side and brought her hand around to her torso. She gripped at the fabric of the silk pyjamas.

"Off," she whispered.

Victoria didn't hesitate and hastily unbuttoned the top with her free hand, the other clutching Holly to her. Holly tried to help, and they chuckled when they both reached the final button and tried to undo it, causing the task to take twice as long.

"I've missed you," Victoria whispered. "Not just this, all of you."

"I feel the same way." Holly got up and straddled Victoria as she tugged off her tank top. She tossed it to the floor and leaned forward to separate the two sides of the pyjama top. She peppered Victoria's neck, breasts, and torso with kisses.

Victoria's hands went to Holly's hips and firmly held her in place as she rolled her head from side to side and gasped at the sensations Holly's lips trailed behind them.

"Never leave again," Victoria muttered. "Stay with me."

"Always," Holly promised between kisses.

Victoria's hips twitched upwards, and Holly could tell that she was eager. She couldn't blame her; she felt exactly the same way, but she also wanted to take her time and demonstrate to Victoria just how much she loved her.

Suddenly she sat up, forcing Holly to do the same.

"I'm serious," Victoria said. "I can't be apart from you again."

Holly swept Victoria's hair back with both hands. "You won't have to. You'll have to forcibly remove me if you want me to leave."

Victoria smiled. "Never."

She tilted her body, and Holly fell to the mattress. Victoria kicked off her pyjama trousers, and Holly did the same. A second later, Victoria lay down, and they faced each other, coming together in a kiss that had precisely zero finesse. Holly knew neither of them were going to last long. They simply needed to be together, to prove their love for one another, and to put the frightening thoughts of being apart well and truly behind them.

CHAPTER THIRTY-EIGHT

Two Months Later

"GOOD MORNING," Victoria greeted her family as she entered the kitchen.

Holly smiled at her, Alexia grunted from her cereal bowl, and Hugo nodded his head half-heartedly while maintaining his gaze on his iPhone. It was the usual Sunday morning breakfast.

Except this was not going to be like any other Sunday. She'd decided that today would be the day.

She poured herself a mug of coffee, picked up an orange, and walked over to the table. She kissed the top of Alexia's head before she sat down.

"Mom, can we go to the Guggenheim this week? They have an exhibition I want to see," Alexia asked.

"Later in the week maybe; it will depend on how the court case goes," Victoria told her. "Mommy needs to make sure she's available in case the judge needs to hear her tell her side of the story for the ten thousandth time. Because judges don't understand that people have busy lives."

"And judges want to make sure that everyone gets a fair trial," Holly added.

Victoria picked up the entertainment section of the newspaper and started to flip through it. She had no intention of responding to that remark.

"But you won't go to jail, right?" Alexia asked.

Victoria looked up and frowned. "Why would I?"

Alexia shrugged and returned to her cereal, swirling the spoon around the milk, the few floating pieces of whatever sugary cereal Holly had allowed her to eat being pulverised in the process.

Holly put her arm around Alexia's shoulders and leaned in close. "No jail could hold your mother, you know that."

"They'd send her back after a couple of hours," Hugo added.

Victoria looked from Holly to Hugo, not knowing who to tell off first.

"True," Alexia agreed.

Victoria huffed and turned her attention back to her paper.

"Your mom isn't in any trouble," Holly continued. "She's just helping everyone so they know exactly what happened so that everything can be sorted out."

"The paper said money was stolen from *Arrival* and they made it look like Mom did it," Alexia said.

Victoria looked up again. She hadn't known that Alexia was actively reading about what had happened. They'd given her a brief overview of the situation, but Victoria knew the papers liked to twist things for a more entertaining read.

"That's true," Holly said, "but she didn't do anything, and everyone knows that. She's just helping out so the judge knows what happened."

"Promise?" Alexia asked. She looked up at Holly, her brows furrowed.

"Pinkie promise," Holly agreed. She held her hand up, her little finger outstretched.

Alexia matched the move, and they shook with their little fingers. Victoria smiled to herself and looked back at the paper.

She'd agonised for weeks over the perfect way to ask Holly to marry her, eventually consulting with Gideon who had talked her down from some of her more apparently outlandish ideas.

Admittedly, hiring the New York Choral Society to serenade them was overkill.

It was Alexia who brought a sudden end to most of her plans. Just three nights ago, Alexia had demanded an emergency meeting with her. They'd sat in Victoria's office, Alexia taking her chair and Victoria relegated the guest chair for some reason. Alexia had told her, in no uncertain terms, that it was high time she proposed to Holly.

She said she agreed, and Alexia had let out the almightiest sigh of relief and told her she needed to get on with it and "put a ring on it." Victoria patiently explained that she was preparing something because she wanted it to be perfect for Holly.

Alexia had made a face. She explained that Holly didn't like being the centre of attention, nor did she like big, flashy shows of affection. Which was absolutely right. Victoria realised that evening that she had been cruising blindly towards creating a perfect proposal for someone else, but certainly not for Holly Carter.

And so, she'd ended up asking her nine-year-old daughter for advice on proposing to her girlfriend, which was quite surreal and not at all where she expected to find herself at forty-eight years of age.

"I was thinking," she said as she tapped her finger on the paper. "Maybe a trip to Central Park?"

"I was actually thinking of Brooklyn Botanic Garden," Holly said.

She paused, not expecting Holly to have turned down a trip to one of her favourite places. She considered the change and decided it wouldn't really impact her plans, which were woefully simple. She just hoped Alexia was right about keeping things modest.

"Of course, sounds lovely."

"Sounds boring," Hugo said, on cue.

Of course, she'd already discussed the matter with him. She needed both of the children to agree to vanish for an agreed amount of time to give her the opportunity to propose.

"Yeah, Yawnsville," Alexia agreed.

"Then why don't you two come with us for a short walk and then you can do something else?" Holly suggested. "At least get some exercise."

"Fine," Hugo muttered, attention back on his phone.

"Okay, but not a long walk," Alexia bartered.

The children bowed out after just twenty minutes, which was all it took for Holly and Victoria to get to the Bluebell Wood.

The butterflies that danced amongst the flowers were nothing in comparison to the ones in Victoria's stomach. She'd attempted to remain upbeat, so Holly wouldn't notice that she was going through some kind of crisis. She had no idea if it was working or not because everything seemed to be moving in slow motion.

She knew she had to get on with it and find out if Holly would even consider spending her life with her before she gave herself some terrible medical condition brought on by ridiculously high amounts of stress.

Thankfully, it was a peaceful and quiet day in the garden, and the Bluebell Wood was completely empty.

"This is so nice," Holly said. "Just what I wanted for today."

"Likewise," Victoria agreed. Her hand gripped the small jewellery box in her coat pocket, and she rubbed her thumb gently over the velvety material.

She'd had a speech planned out, but it had somehow vanished from her mind and she was left with absolutely nothing. For someone who had spent their entire life editing a magazine, words weren't supposed to be difficult to come across, but today it seemed impossible.

"Can we sit down?" Holly asked, gesturing to a beautifully carved bench.

"Of course." A rest was probably a good idea. She was struggling to catch her breath, such were her nerves.

They both sat down, and Victoria looked out over the thousands of bluebells planted under oak, birch, and beech trees. It looked perfect. Now she just needed to find her words.

"With everything that happened recently," Holly said, "I've realised some things."

"Me too," Victoria agreed, suddenly remembering the start of her proposal speech now that the words had somehow come from Holly's mouth.

"I don't know if I tell you often enough how much I love you," Holly said, taking her hand. "I know I say it a lot, but I need you to know that I mean it and also how strong that love for you is. Being apart from you was painful, and I never want to do that again."

"Neither do I," Victoria agreed readily. She knew she had to get into the conversation and say something soon before the moment passed.

"The thing is," Holly continued, "I know you think I'm young, but I know what I want from life. And that's you. And our family. I want that, and I want it forever. And I want the world to know about it."

Victoria's eyes widened as she realised that Holly was proposing to her.

"Wait." The word fell from Victoria's lips.

Holly stopped. Her cheeks were flushed, and she licked her lips, fear in her eyes.

"No. No." Victoria stood up. "No, *I* was supposed to say this. I had it planned. I just didn't have time to say it because you wanted to sit down, and I... I just needed another couple of moments."

She pinched the bridge of her nose. This was ridiculous. Her simple proposal had gone completely off the rails. This wouldn't have happened if she'd had that man from New

Jersey release a hundred white doves. No, Holly wouldn't have been able to sneak in her own proposal before they came flying overhead.

Holly burst out laughing.

Victoria slowly turned to look down at her. "Is something amusing you?"

"Are you seriously miffed that I'm proposing to you before you get a chance to propose to me?" Holly asked, still laughing.

"Yes! I've thought about this for weeks, the planning. And then the booking, and then the cancelling because skywriters are contributing to climate change. And flash mobs, where do you hire them? They are all in California. Try to find a flash mob in New York, I dare you. Then Ellen said she'd help, but, really, if she is going to continue with that awful clothing line of hers then I don't think I can continue to be friends with her at all."

Holly stood up and grabbed her hands, a huge, ridiculous grin still on her face. "I'm sorry, deeply sorry, that I commandeered your proposal," she said without even a trace of real apology in her voice. "Please, do continue. I promise I won't interrupt your proposal with my own."

Victoria sighed. "Well, you've said most of what I wanted to say."

"Then how about we don't use words?" Holly suggested. She pulled Victoria closer and gave her the gentlest peck on the lips. Followed by another, and then another. Finally, Victoria caved in and returned the kiss.

They wrapped their arms around each other and held on tightly. Victoria opened her mouth and met Holly's tongue with her own. It wasn't quite how she'd pictured the proposal, French kissing in Brooklyn, but it seemed to be going well.

She pulled away.

"Marry me," she said, more of a demand than a request.

"Of course," Holly said.

She fumbled with the box in her pocket before opening it and showing it to Holly, hoping that the plain and simple band with the tastefully cut square diamond, which was at least five times smaller than she's intended before consulting Gideon, would do.

Holly gasped. "That's beautiful, Victoria. And far, far too expensive."

"Nonsense. I've been embezzling from *Arrival* for years," Victoria deadpanned.

Holly laughed again and pulled her into another kiss.

PATREON

I adore publishing. There's a wonderful thrill that comes from crafting a manuscript and then releasing it to the world. Especially when you are writing woman loving woman characters. I'm blessed to receive messages from readers all over the world who are thrilled to discover characters and scenarios that resemble their lives.

Books are entertaining escapism, but they are also reinforcement that we are not alone in our struggles. I'm passionate about writing books that people can identify with. Books that are accessible to all and show that love—and acceptance—can be found no matter who you are.

I've been lucky enough to have published books that have been best-sellers and even some award-winners. While I'm still quite a new author, I have plans to write many, many more novels. However, writing, editing, and marketing books take up a lot of time... and writing full-time is a treadmill-like existence, especially in a very small niche market like mine.

Don't get me wrong, I feel very grateful and lucky to be

able to live the life I do. But being a full-time author in a small market means never being able to stop and work on developing my writing style, it means rarely having the time or budget to properly market my books, it means immediately picking up the next project the moment the previous has finished.

This is why I have set up a Patreon account. With Patreon, you can donate a small amount each month to enable me to hop off of my treadmill for a while in order to reach my goals. Goals such as exploring better marketing options, developing my writing craft, and investigating writing articles and screenplays.

My Patreon page is a place for exclusive first looks at new works, insight into upcoming projects, Q&A sessions, as well as special gifts and dedications. I'm also pleased to give all of my Patreon subscribers access to **exclusive short stories** which have been written just for patrons. There are tiers to suit all budgets.

My readers are some of the kindest and most supportive people I have met, and I appreciate every book borrow or purchase. With the added support of Patreon, I hope to be able to develop my writing career in order to become a better author as well as level up my marketing strategy to help my books to reach a wider audience.

https://www.patreon.com/aeradley

REVIEWS

I sincerely hope you enjoyed reading this book.

If you did, I would greatly appreciate a short review on your favourite book website.

Reviews are crucial for any author, and even just a line or two can make a huge difference.

ABOUT THE AUTHOR

Amanda Radley had no desire to be a writer but accidentally became an award-winning, bestselling author.

She gave up a marketing career in order to make stuff up for a living instead. She claims the similarities are startling.

She describes herself as a Wife. Traveller. Tea Drinker. Biscuit Eater. Animal Lover. Master Pragmatist. Procrastinator. Theme Park Fan.

Connect with Amanda
www.amandaradley.com

FITTING IN

2020 Amazon Kindle Storyteller Finalist

Starting a new job is hard. Especially if you're the boss's daughter

Heather Bailey has been in charge of Silver Arches, the prestigious London shopping centre, for several years. Financial turmoil brings a new investor to secure the future and Heather finds herself playing office politics with the notoriously difficult entrepreneur Leo Flynn. Walking a fine line between standing her ground and being willing to accept change, Heather has her work cut out for her.

When Leo demands that his daughter is found a job at Silver Arches; things become even harder.

Scarlett Flynn has never fit in. Not in the army, not in her father's firm, not even in her own family. So starting work at Silver Arches won't be any different, will it?

A heartwarming exploration of the art of fitting in.

GOING UP

2020 Selfies Finalist

A ruthless executive. A destitute woman. Both on the way up.

Selina Hale is on her way to the top. She's been working towards a boardroom position on the thirteenth floor for her entire career. And no one is going to get in her way. Not her clueless boss, her soon to be ex-wife, and most certainly not the homeless person who has moved into the car park at work.

Kate Morgan fell through the cracks in a broken support system and found herself destitute. Determined and strong-willed, she's not about to accept help from a mean business woman who can't even remember the names of her own nephews.

As their lives continue to intertwine, they have no choice but to work together and follow each other on their journey up.

SECOND CHANCES

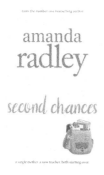

Bad childhood memories start to resurface when Hannah Hall's daughter Rosie begins school. To make matters more complicated, Hannah has been steadfastly ignoring the obvious truth that Rosie is intellectually gifted and wise beyond her years.

In the crumbling old school she meets Rosie's new teacher Alice Spencer who has moved from the city to teach in the small coastal town of Fairlight.

Alice immediately sees Rosie's potential and embarks on developing an educational curriculum to suit Rosie's needs, to Hannah's dismay.

Teacher and mother clash over what's best for young Rosie.

Will they be able to compromise? Will Hannah finally open up to someone about her own damaged upbringing?

And will they be able to ignore the sparks that fly whenever they are in the same room?

Printed in Great Britain
by Amazon

26519964R00152